WANTED: A BABY BY THE SHEIKH

SHEIKH

DESERT KINGS, BOOK 6

DIANA FRASER

BAY BOOKS

Wanted: A Baby by the Sheikh
by Diana Fraser

© 2015 Diana Fraser
Print Edition
ISBN 978-1927323250

"You walked away from our wedding and kept on walking. And I hear nothing from you for a year, except a trail of credit card charges. Now you return saying you want our baby. What the hell is going on, Taina?" But Finnish heiress, Taina, can't answer Prince Daidan's question without destroying his world. So Daidan comes up with a proposal of his own...

—Desert Kings—
Wanted: A Wife for the Sheikh
The Sheikh's Bargain Bride
The Sheikh's Lost Lover
Awakened by the Sheikh
Claimed by the Sheikh
Wanted: A Baby by the Sheikh

Print Edition

For more information about this author, visit:
http://www.dianafraser.net

❀ Created with Vellum

CONTENTS

*D*espite the icy wind, Taina Mustonen remained on deck, watching the island grow ever larger. She pushed the collar of her white coat up high around her ears and mouth, so only her eyes were exposed. She reassured herself that it was the cold that made them water.

Behind her, the glittering lights of Helsinki pierced the dark night like cut diamonds. She glanced at them briefly, as if for strength, before turning once more to the island. There was no point in looking back. She breathed deeply of the frigid air and looked up at the house whose windows were dark, save one, where a red light stuttered around the silhouette of a man—her estranged husband, Prince Daidan ibn Saleh al-Fulan.

She swallowed. He was waiting for her.

Her gaze remained fixed on the dark shape. She couldn't see the details of his face, but her memory filled in the gaps. He'd be watching her with that narrowed gaze that used to make her pulse race. Used to? It still did, even though she couldn't see him. But she wasn't here to rekindle what might have been. He was a businessman and so a business proposition was what she'd give him.

The hired boat pulled alongside the jetty and she quickly walked up the steps toward the house. She tried hard to suppress the memories of a lonely childhood spent wistfully looking out from her glass-walled home, toward the lights of the city. She failed and paused for a moment to gather herself, looking up, above the house and tree line to the irregular shape of the old castle that dominated the small island. But that brought forth only more memories she'd prefer to forget. Her gaze fell to the long low house that nestled amongst the trees. Still the one light—in the lounge she realized—still the shadow of the man she'd come to see, still the flicker of nerves which she had to contain if she wanted to succeed. She took a deep breath and walked up to the wide sweep of steps that led to the house.

She hesitated before entering the front door, feeling she should knock at her childhood home. Stupid. It was still half hers after all, even if she chose not to live in it.

She pushed open the heavy door and paused, expecting to be greeted by the housekeeper, but she didn't appear. Daidan must have dismissed her for the night. Or perhaps for good. It was none of her business anymore, she reminded herself.

She took a long calming breath before entering the lounge, willing the buzz of nerves to subside. She could do this. She'd emerged from worse situations. What could he do to her that she hadn't already done to herself? She kept her gaze lowered as she closed the door quietly behind her.

"You took your time."

His voice—as powerful and distinctive as ever with its foreign edge—shot straight to her heart, jump-starting it into a staccato rhythm that sent adrenaline surging through her body.

She turned to find he'd moved from the window and was

now standing before the log fire, legs planted squarely apart as if expecting a fight. She could barely decipher the details of his tall silhouette but she felt his eyes upon her, as hot as the flames that framed him.

She walked briskly to the sofa, channeling the energy into movement, praying that he wouldn't detect her weakness. For Daidan, weakness was something to exploit.

"I had things to do."

"Like waste my money."

She sat on the soft leather sofa and slowly crossed one long, elegant leg over the other, knowing he wouldn't fail to notice.

"My darling husband, I believe that was the deal. You receive half my inheritance and I receive, let me think? Why yes, nothing but an annual income to play with."

There was a long pause in which she held his cold gaze.

"Drink?"

She nodded. While he poured the drinks, she allowed herself to scan his face, once so dear. The spare, strong bone structure of someone who was too self-controlled hadn't changed, nor had his striking coloring of rich nutmeg skin and nearly black eyes. He was still the exotic sheikh in a land of pale Finns. But there were changes. The groove between his brows was more deeply furrowed than she remembered and his mouth was set in a firm line, as if the tense expression never left him now. She couldn't meet his gaze as he handed her the glass of whiskey.

"Thank you. What shall we drink to?" Her voice sounded too high, strained.

He returned to his position before the fire. "How about the truth for a change?" His eyes narrowed until their dark brown tones had disappeared leaving only a streak of dark charcoal. "Why *have* you returned? Why now? What is it you want?"

"The truth?" She allowed her mouth to quirk into a smile that held no laughter. "I wonder if you'd know it if it came and slapped you in the face." She brought the glass to her lips —watching his gaze dip to her mouth—and slowly sipped the whiskey.

"You, Taina, are the only person who's ever had the nerve to slap me in the face." He knocked back a mouthful of his drink and a silence fell that only the crackle of the fire relieved. He swallowed and she watched the movement of his Adam's apple with fascination. He looked down at her suddenly and she looked away, as if caught out. "Like the spoilt child you were."

"I'm surprised you didn't slap me back."

"So am I." He held her gaze without blinking. The shadows from the firelight darted over his face, changing and distorting his features until she no longer recognized him. "I should have done it. Maybe then you'd have grown up more quickly."

"Convenient—for you to believe anyone who disagrees with you is immature."

"In your case, I'm right." He held her gaze for one long, silent moment. "You still haven't told me why you've returned, what it is you want."

It was too soon. She shifted in her seat, recrossing her legs to distract him. "Tell me, Daidan, how's business?"

His frown deepened. "Business? Since when have you been interested in business?"

"Since now. The latest report from the mine sounds promising."

His face relaxed as she moved onto the one thing that truly interested him—the diamond mine in northern Finland they co-owned. "It is. Early reports look to be outstanding. The new equipment and mining standards we've implemented have been well-received internationally. But…"

She raised an elegant eyebrow. "But?"

"But, nothing. You still haven't told me why you're here."

"All in good time. Tell me about the 'but'."

"Why do you want to know?" The guard was in place again.

She shrugged lightly. "I don't know. Maybe because I co-own it? And would have had one hundred percent ownership if you hadn't persuaded my father to sell you half."

He gritted his teeth and a muscle twitched in his jaw. Seconds passed before he continued. "We've had a few problems. The Russians aren't pleased with our improved safety records. It has highlighted the bad conditions in their own mines and they've lost some contracts to us. And they're not happy. I've had to put extra security measures in place." He shrugged. "But we're expanding as planned and our international reputation will be cemented with the launch of the new jewelry collection."

"You're using the jewelry designs Mama was working on before she died?" She never talked about either her mother or her mother's work, but she had to know.

He nodded. "Yes, they'll give us the credibility we need. I've hired a new design team to complete them."

"Good, they're too beautiful not to use."

"Indeed. So, are you going to tell me what this is all about yet?" He held up his hand before she could answer. "Wait, I think I know. You realize how much you love me and miss me and want to begin again." Before she could answer, his lip curled in disdain. "As if… No, it's something different you want. Something's happened. I can see it in your eyes. Tell me."

His obvious indifference to her was like a knife to her heart. But she'd be damned if she'd show it. "Please, keep on guessing, it's so entertaining. I wonder what you'll come up with next?"

His eyes darkened. "No more games. We're not at one of your cocktail parties. Tell me what the hell you want from me."

It was now or never. "Okay, you're right. I do want something."

"What?"

She channeled her tension into a smile: tight at first but with focus it transformed into the mocking smile she desired. "I've decided to keep my side of the bargain."

That caught his attention. No one else would have noticed the change in his expression. It was so slight. But she did. It was there in the quick flare in his eyes, in the brief pinched frown. But nothing else moved, not his mouth, his body, nothing. But did the slight change simply denote surprise or something more?

"And which bargain might that be?" His voice was ice-cold.

"To have our child. I produce a baby and you gain complete control of the mine, just as you and my father had arranged."

He didn't speak.

She looked up and hoped her glittering eyes wouldn't betray her. "Surely you haven't forgotten the bargain you and Papa made shortly before his death?" she continued. "The bargain which Papa's lawyer informed me of on our wedding day. I knew we talked about children but, silly me, I thought you just wanted a family with me. Pure and simple." She looked up at him and at that moment, wondered if she could continue without breaking down. "But nothing's pure and simple with you, or Papa, is it? You'd both agreed I should have a baby with you. A child in return for total control of the mine."

"You've returned because you want to have a child," he repeated as a statement, as if unable to understand.

She nodded and focused her attention on brushing her fingertips over the soft pile of the arctic white cushion, noticing how her fingers were so tense that their tips quivered. She sunk them deeper so that he wouldn't notice. She steeled herself and looked up at him. "Yes, I want our child."

His gaze was narrowed and he shook his head in disbelief. "You walked away from our wedding, just walked away and kept walking while I waited for you, not knowing. And I heard nothing from you except a trail of bank transactions, credit card bills, for over a year. Now, without explanation you return saying you want our baby. What the hell is going on, Taina?"

A spark of anger at this simplistic version of events chased away the nerves. "You know full well why I left."

At least he had the grace to look uncomfortable. "I thought you knew everything."

"I knew I wanted to marry you and I'd believed you wanted to marry me. Just those two things were all I knew."

"Life is never that simple."

"Yes, I knew life—my life in particular—wasn't simple, and yet I still believed it could be." She shook her head. "Naïve." She looked down at her drink and swilled it around in irritation at the memory. "I was stupid. I should have realized I'd been sold by my father to the highest bidder. When I found out, I even accepted it until I discovered giving you a child was also part of the deal. I drew the line at that."

"But now?"

"Now..." She met his steady gaze. "*Now*, I've changed my mind."

"Why?"

She should tell him straight away. He wanted honesty and she could be honest. It'd just been a long time since she *had* been. His expression was both curious and mocking. These she could deal with. But there was one emotion she couldn't risk seeing in his eyes—pity.

"I can't see it matters. I'm here to keep my side of the bargain." She forced herself to look him in the eye. "If you're no longer interested, just say so and I'll leave. But a child is what you always said you wanted." She couldn't show him how much she, too, now wanted it.

With cool deliberation he placed his glass on the mantelpiece, his long dark fingers caressing the crystal momentarily, just as they'd used to caress her. Then he came and stood before her, searching her face as if trying to understand her. In that moment she felt the full blast of her connection with him. He didn't touch her—he didn't have to. From the first time they'd met it had been the same. He only had to look at her with those dark eyes—full of the heat of the desert rather than the ice of the north—for her to want him. Despite all that had gone before, it was the same now.

She tried to control the warmth that spread through her body, but she shifted her stockinged legs one against the other instinctively, and his gaze dropped to her legs. When his gaze returned to hers, it was hot with desire. But instead of acting on it, as he had in the past, he shook his head and walked away.

He flung the window open wide, sending in a blast of snowy, late spring air, which set the flames in the fire surging. She watched the snowflakes drift into the room and settle momentarily on the leather sofa before melting, leaving a darkened patch like blood on the honey-colored leather. She shivered.

He turned his back to the window and she dredged up every last bit of courage, rose from her chair and walked over to him. She could smell his aftershave and something more… something indefinably him. It made her mouth water. "It's what you wanted," she repeated.

For a moment she thought she had him as he inclined his head to hers. "No longer," he whispered into her ear, flaring a trail of goosebumps down her spine.

She hadn't come this far to risk what she wanted so much. She laid her hand on his arm and looked up at him from beneath lowered lashes. "I don't believe you." He glanced at her hand and then back into her eyes with an unchanging expression.

He took her hand and for one moment she thought he was going to thread his fingers through hers and pull her to him until she was held tight in his embrace. Just as he had done whenever they used to meet, before they married. But he dropped her hand. "For some reason you've returned. I don't kid myself it's for me. I don't even know if it's for a child. I don't know whether you're able to tell the truth anymore."

"What do you mean? I've always told you the truth." For a moment she faltered. She'd never lied exactly, but maybe she'd withheld the truth.

His lip curled with disdain. "Like when you didn't turn up to that function in New York you'd agreed to attend before you left me?" The memory of why she couldn't do as she'd agreed made her turn away. *There*, right *there*, was the limit to her truth.

"It wasn't like that."

He scoffed. "No, I'm sure it wasn't."

She turned back to him. "Look…" But she could see there would be no point in arguing, no point in saying anything when the truth could destroy the world he'd carefully created. She sighed. She should go. There was no point in staying. She walked over to the sofa and picked up her coat. "I shouldn't have returned."

She didn't hear him come up behind her but his touch halted her mid-stride. "You came because you needed to.

Now tell me why." He slid his hand down her arm and grabbed hold of her wrist and pulled her to face him. "Why?" he asked again, his tone softer, more cajoling now.

She swallowed. "I'm telling the truth, Daidan. I want a baby."

"Why do you want a baby so badly all of a sudden?"

"It's not sudden. It's… I can't explain."

"Because you don't understand? It is natural, *habibti*. You are a woman."

She nearly choked at his arrogant sexism and was about to contradict him before she stopped herself. There was no point in telling him he was wrong because he'd only want to know the truth and there was no way she was telling him that. She nodded slowly. "I expect that's it."

He stroked her face once, as if needing to check that she was really there, and she closed her eyes against his devastating touch. Please God, let him be satisfied with that.

"Open your eyes, *habibti*."

She pressed them closed more tightly. He knew. But there was no avoiding it now. She opened them to see his eyes as intense as ever, probing into the very heart of her.

"There's something more. Tell me."

"Isn't it enough that I want our baby?" She tried to pull away but his hold on her hand tightened.

"No. I want to know why. Why now? What's happened to make you change your mind?"

She shrugged stiffly. "It was never that I was against having a baby, just that I didn't want it to be a requirement of our marriage."

"I understand that. But you're still not telling me something. Tell me the truth. Why do you want our baby? Why now?"

She licked her suddenly dry lips, unable to draw her gaze away from his. "I…" She couldn't say the words. She hadn't rehearsed them, she'd forgotten how perceptive he was, and how determined.

"Go on," he gentled. He tilted his head quizzically to one side. "What could happen to make you realize you want a child? Did a friend have a baby?"

She shook her head.

"It couldn't be the ticking clock… you are still too young. So not the presence of a baby, not the passing of time. What else could make you want something so much, that you'd risk the humiliation of me declining? This need for a child must be strong."

She nodded.

"Tell me." He stroked her hand gently and she remembered how he used to do that when they were courting. When the slightest touch would stir desires she'd never even imagined.

For the first time she suddenly thought that maybe, just maybe, he'd understand. That she could tell him and he'd think no worse of her, and that everything would be okay. And suddenly she wanted *that* more than anything. She opened her mouth to speak but he narrowed his eyes.

"You're afraid. You're afraid of my response." The gentle touch on her hand turned into a tight grip. "What the hell happened to you, Taina?"

And in that instant she knew she couldn't tell him. It would only make everything so much worse than it already was.

She pulled her hand away from his and walked away. "You're imagining things, Daidan. I simply want a child. As you say, it's natural in a woman. You're my husband, and this is my home. A year away and I realize I want to be in my home." She shrugged. "All quite natural."

"You expect me to welcome you back with open arms

because on a whim you have decided you want a baby. What happens when you grow bored with the baby?"

"That won't happen."

She must have conveyed her seriousness to him because he nodded slowly.

"So, what's your answer?"

"My answer? That depends."

"Stop playing games, Daidan."

"You accuse *me* of playing games?"

She grunted with frustration and put on her coat. "I'm going. I've obviously wasted my time." She picked up her bag and was half-way to the door before he spoke.

"I didn't say I wasn't interested in your proposal."

She stopped dead in her tracks and turned back to him. "I thought disapproval and anger probably indicated that."

He walked slowly over to her. "Then you thought wrong." He picked up a scarf she'd accidentally left on the sofa and hooked it around her neck, his hands dragging down each side of the soft cashmere. "You want to bargain? Then I will. But not your way. You can have the child you want. You can return to your life in Finland, to the family home."

She tensed as she waited for him to finish. "Go on."

He smiled briefly. "Most people would have thought that was it. But you know me too well."

"I've tried hard to forget, but it's proved more difficult than I imagined. I guess when someone uses you with such ease, when someone tricks you into a marriage, all for their own gain, then it's hard to forget."

His face hardened. "You believe what you want to believe. You always have and no doubt you always will." He paced away from her as if he couldn't bear to be near her. "As I said you can have the property and land your parents left you, and you can have the child you apparently desire so much. But, in return, I want you to work."

"Work? Doing what? Typing your letters?"

"I want you to work in your family jewelry business—in Kielo. In the ten years since your mother died, the company has lost its edge. I'm re-launching it with a new team of designers as a showcase for our diamonds. You trained as a designer and simply being a Mustonen will help our marketing."

"It was so useful that I never changed my name after we married. No doubt another part of the agreement between you and my father about which I knew nothing."

"Yes, it is useful," he said, deliberately ignoring her sarcasm. "It's a prestigious name in Finland, a name that will help the company's branding as a reliable family firm. A firm in which you will work."

She shook her head. "You are joking, aren't you? What do I know about the business? My design training was for show only. I've never used it. My father brought me up to marry and breed. I've done the former, now I'm here to begin a family. That's the only role I've been raised for."

"I want you to work on the public launch of the diamond company," he continued as if she hadn't spoken. "The advertising agency says the company needs someone to represent the company brand... someone like you. Someone beautiful, someone well-connected, someone to be the face of the company. You do this for me, for our company, and you can have your child."

"And I suppose you still want one hundred percent ownership of the mine?"

"No. No, I don't. We'll continue to own it jointly and it'll be inherited by our children. Because, Taina, if you have a child by me we will remain together."

"Just one big happy family."

Again he ignored her sarcasm. "I don't see why not. And *if* we're not"—he shrugged—"we will at least appear to be, for the sake of the children. I suggest you accept my offer, Taina. Because there will be no other."

It was as she'd imagined—at least some form of family life, as her parents had given her. What she *hadn't* imagined was his declining 100% ownership of the mine. Was he trying to show he regretted what had happened? She also hadn't imagined becoming involved with her mother's company. That would be harder for her than Daidan thought—and not for the reasons she'd given. But she had no choice but to accept his offer. The heartache remained. She guessed it always would. But she had to try to ease it, try to heal, to begin again.

She nodded. He held out his hand and she took it, closing her eyes briefly as his large warm hand engulfed her slender one.

"Do you agree?"

"I agree."

"Tomorrow morning. My office."

He turned away and went back to his stance in front of the fire, just as he'd been when she first entered.

She walked away, out the door, and along the jetty to the boat. She didn't look back this time. Shivering under her coat, she narrowed her eyes against the dancing lights of Helsinki. Coming ever nearer. Her future. And with it, the child she so desperately wanted. Something to stem the heartache that throbbed continually, deep down, never easing. Time hadn't done it. She hoped a child would do it— fill this aching void.

But it wouldn't be easy because Daidan had been correct. She wasn't telling him everything. And if she still cared for him, even a little bit, it would have to stay that way. Because her secret had the potential to destroy his whole world. And she couldn't do that to him.

CHAPTER 2

*D*aidan swept walked into his office suite in the 1930s modernist office building and immediately turned to his assistant. "Where is she?" It was always his first thought on waking and his last before he went to sleep. He doubted he'd ever lose that sense of insecurity. At least now he could ask the question and receive an accurate answer.

"I gave her the corner desk, sir."

He strode over to the internal window and looked across the open-plan space to where Taina sat. He grunted softly. She looked more at home here than he ever would, despite what he felt. She fitted the building with its clean white lines and beautiful detailing. While he? He might have turned the companies around, made them more profitable than Taina's father ever dreamed of, but with his dark looks and dislike of socializing he'd always be a foreigner.

"What's she doing?"

His assistant looked suitably inscrutable although Daidan realized Aarne must be wondering what the hell was going on. But it didn't matter—he paid him enough not to gossip.

"She asked for some Board meeting documents which I took to her."

"Hm." Daidan turned away from the sight of her back—flawlessly clothed in the arctic white she favored. She looked as coolly beautiful as always with her blond hair, slender figure, and exquisite clothes. "What kind of Board papers?"

"Everything from the mining reports to Kielo's accounts."

"And has she visited Kielo's premises—The Warehouse—as I'd instructed?"

"No, sir."

Daidan grunted. "And does she know about the interview in an hour?"

"Yes, sir."

"Make sure she's prepped for it."

As his assistant went out into the main office, Daidan sat, turned his laptop to face him and began scrolling through his messages. There were emails about the upcoming launch, about the mine, about everything except the one thing he suddenly realized he was looking for—a message from her. He pushed the laptop away and sighed. They hadn't exchanged two words since their meeting on the island the day before. He'd had a breakfast meeting and hadn't been here to see her arrive. He wondered if he'd pushed her too hard. But it was for her own good. It was time she realized just how capable and talented she was. So he was going to do to her what his father had done to him when he refused to learn to swim—throw her in the deep end. It would do her good, it would do the company good—he glanced at her as she wrinkled her lovely brow in concentration—and it would give him the pleasure of working with her. Because like it or not, he loved her and always would. He rose, irritated by the thought, and called his assistant over once more.

After an hour of barking instructions at the poor assistant, Daidan felt a little better. At least he'd been able to distract himself from the thoughts that had haunted him all night long.

But suddenly they were interrupted—not by a knock on the door, not by the sound of the phone or someone speaking, but by the drift of her perfume across the room. She'd always worn it and he looked up instinctively as he took a deep breath of her fragrance.

Framed by the pale wood of the door surround, she stood poised and cool, not a strand of her short blond hair out of place. He dragged his gaze away from her eyes that stung him with their distance, and dismissed his assistant with a brisk wave of the hand. "What are you doing here? I understand you didn't go to The Warehouse to meet the designers."

She walked across the room and he was unable to take his eyes off her lithe, elegant figure. She'd used to be unaware of the effect she had on men, but he could see from her increased assurance that she was now aware of her movements, even if she didn't accentuate them. Somehow it made the pain just a little bit sharper.

"I thought I'd update myself on some admin here, first. I've been looking through your ideas for the midsummer launch on the island. And the guest list."

"Does it meet with your approval?"

"Yes."

He waited but she didn't elaborate. "Good. And I hear you've been looking through some financial papers."

"Yes. It turns out my father's instinct about you was correct. Mine, possibly not, but how you've turned both companies around in a year is nothing short of miraculous."

"Miracles? Instinct? No, Taina. Your father knew I was the best person to head the company because of my experience working in the Australian diamond industry and my postgrad research."

"And you've made the company your own, just as you always wanted."

"It's what I've worked for my whole adult life. And I always get what I want in the end."

She cocked her head to one side. "Is that right?"

"Absolutely." He steepled his fingers. "Including a continued working relationship with the Aussies which will be extremely profitable for both of us. As I said, I'm the best in the field. That's why Amelia and Mark still want to work with us."

"And yet their names don't appear on the guest list."

"They're not coming. We decided it would be better if we weren't seen to be working too closely together. Why do you ask?"

"No reason."

"Anyway, you need to focus on tweaking the new designs. This launch is too important to mess up. The designs have to be the best. There can be nothing else in the world to match them, nothing else like them. The team has been doing a good job, but there's something subtle lacking."

She raised an elegant eyebrow and desire ignited from nowhere. It was the first thing that he had noticed about her. That cool elegance, that aloofness, that raised eyebrow instead of words. It had got him every time and apparently it still did.

"Here." He pushed the laptop closer toward her. "These are the pieces we have so far."

She brought the laptop even closer and frowned as she focused on the images. He watched her eyes move from one piece to another. Then she looked up at him. "They're good, very good even, but there's something missing."

"Go on."

"They need a central piece to bring the designs into focus, to make them Kielo designs."

He nodded.

"But we have the necklace your grandfather had made—the original Kielo piece. We can use that as the focal point for the collection."

She looked away suddenly, through the wide expanse of sheer floor to ceiling glass windows to the central city and the harbor, dotted with islands, beyond. But before he could ask her what the matter was she'd turned back.

"Anyway, this interview. Aarne tells me it's with Vogue?"

"Yes, the editor will be here any minute."

"Milla, the editor-in-chief? Impressive. And… don't tell me, you want us to appear the perfect loving couple."

He stared at her impassively, hating her sarcastic tone. Hating the fact that she didn't love him and was at no pains to hide it. "No. Not loving. I don't wish you to appear anything other than you are."

"That just leaves 'perfect' then?"

"Yes. Perfect and a couple, representing the glamorous image capable of persuading people to buy our diamonds and our jewelry."

"Easy." She glanced out the window as two cars drew up. "Looks like she's arrived. Tell me, Daidan, what were you going to do if I didn't return? Without me, how were you going to brand the campaign?"

He leaned against the desk. "I'd considered selling the jewelry arm and concentrating on mining diamonds."

She shrugged. "I'm surprised you didn't. Why is that?"

He hesitated. He'd often thought about it, but was unwilling to sever the final connection with Taina. "It made commercial sense to hold on to it in the short term. And besides, I hired a model to become the face of the company." Taina narrowed her eyes, hiding her thoughts. He smiled. "Yes, she had everything… except the family connection.

19

That was the clincher. Pedigree makes such a difference." He couldn't resist the small jibe.

"You hired a model?"

"Yes. She's beautiful. And a very easy person to work with."

"I'm sure," she ground out, and he smiled at her irritation. "You've been connected with just about every eligible, and not eligible, woman in Finland… and overseas."

He smiled. Let her think what she liked. It didn't suit his purposes yet for her to know the truth—that there hadn't been any other woman for him since he'd met her.

"I've paid the model off. We don't need her now because we have you, instead."

"Only if you keep your end of the bargain."

"Of course. Tonight suit you?" For the first time he saw her blanch. "Come on, you didn't think I'd submit to the indignity of providing you with a vial of sperm, did you?"

She shook her head.

"And yet… you hadn't pictured us sleeping together? Tell me, habibti, how exactly did you imagine I'd father our child?"

She licked her lips and it did things to him that it really shouldn't have.

"I'd thought…"

He sat back and crossed his arms. "Yes?"

She looked up at him with those big violet eyes. "I'd thought that—" She cleared her throat. "No, I remembered the times we were together… they were easy, we always…."

"Wanted each other?" he prompted. "And you think that hasn't changed?"

"Has it?"

He opened his mouth to spit out a retort, but no words came. He'd never lied to Taina about anything—maybe he should have—and he wasn't about to start now. "No, it hasn't.

When I look at you, I want to…" He paused. "Let's just say I don't foresee any difficulty. If our past coupling has been anything to go by, I'm sure creating a child won't be too onerous for either of us."

"Not too onerous," she repeated. "Good. And the timing works." She shot him a brief, tight smile, designed to hide her thoughts. "So… shall I come to the island or your apartment?" Her voice had suddenly taken on a husky note.

"I only go the island on the occasional weekend. My apartment is convenient for work. Come to my apartment. I'll have someone pick up your things from the hotel. Yes, come there. Tonight. I'd like that." The words slipped out before he could stop them.

"You would?"

"Why do you sound so surprised?"

"It's just that…"

"We've come to an arrangement. And that arrangement can hardly be acted upon if you continue to live in a hotel. Besides, we have to keep up the happy front, don't we?"

At that moment the door opened and the editor from Vogue entered and they both turned to her as one and smiled. The games had begun.

"So…" Milla, the sharp-eyed editor, looked from Daidan, to Taina and then lingeringly back to Daidan again. "The relaunch of Kielo diamonds." She clicked on the digital recorder, crossed her legs and leaned toward him. "Tell me about it."

Taina glanced at Daidan. "What would you like to know, Milla?"

"So much, Daidan…" she murmured. "So much. But I'll begin with the company. My research shows it goes back to your grandfather, Taina?"

Taina cleared her throat. "Yes, he founded it. He owned land in northern Finland in the diamond fields which extend into Russia, into Ukrelia. He began mining on a small scale to begin with, where the diamonds were largest and most easily accessible."

"Ah, and that would have been when he discovered the original Kielo diamond." Milla slid a photo across the table. "One of the most fabled in the world. A collector's dream."

"And it will remain a dream," interjected Daidan. "The piece was made into a necklace which my wife now owns." They exchanged guarded glances. "And it'll form the center-piece of our collection."

The reporter gave a low whistle. "The collection which will re-launch Kielo jewelry designs, a showcase for your family's diamond mine. I hope you'll have guards on hand!"

"Oh yes. The combined value of all the pieces will be in excess of ten million dollars. So we'll be working with replicas most of the time. The originals will remain under lock and key in Helsinki except for the launch of course."

"But you'll give the press a viewing?" She smiled. "Maybe that's something we could discuss over dinner?"

Daidan smiled back. "My wife and I would be delighted. We have plans tonight, but perhaps another evening?"

It seemed the editor was less delighted that Daidan's wife would be joining them. She turned a cooler face to Taina. "And Taina, so nice to see you back. Tell me how was the Caribbean, or was it Aspen, or the Maldives?" She screwed up her face in mock confusion. "Where was it you went? Rumor had you placed in just about every hotspot over the past twelve months."

Taina licked her suddenly dry mouth, unable to think how to respond. Daidan came to her rescue.

He leaned forward, his hands gathered loosely between

his knees and cast the reporter an intent look. "I don't think we're here to discuss Taina's holiday, do you, Milla?"

The reporter blushed and stammered. "Of course. So… tell me what it is you're most looking forward to about the launch?"

Taina nodded to Daidan, she was on firmer ground now. "It's a culmination of years of work. First by my father who sadly passed away before he could see the results of his labors." She glanced at Daidan. "And then by Daidan who's taken it beyond my father's imaginings."

"And your mother?"

There was another awkward pause. Her mother's death had been hushed up but Taina knew that rumors as to what really happened were plentiful. "The launch will mark ten years since her death. And it will be her pieces which will provide the focus of the launch. And so, of course, it'll be a very special moment for me." She glanced at Daidan, determined not to let the other woman have even a small victory. "For both of us." She extended her hand to Daidan who took it and brought it to his lips and kissed it. There was a flash as someone took a photograph.

"As you can see, Milla, it's going to be very much a family affair," said Daidan.

Then he looked back at Taina with a warmth as if he'd been touched by her answers. They were only the truth but maybe he hadn't been expecting the truth. And with just that one look suddenly she thought things might just work out between them.

DAIDAN OPENED the door for her and stepped aside. "Dinner went well tonight, I thought. The team seemed very upbeat."

He watched her enter the apartment which he'd bought

after she'd left and look around. "Yes, they were enthusiastic. They're going to be fun to work with." She walked up to first one painting and then another and then glanced around the entire space. "These are all new."

"You didn't expect me to take your artwork, did you? After you left I put everything of yours, everything of the family's, into storage."

"I noticed you kept my mother's painting of me. It was in the lounge, on the island."

He shrugged. "Must have escaped my notice."

"Of course." She turned back to the new painting and examined it closely. "It's beautiful."

He came up behind her and gently touched her shoulders. He hesitated a moment waiting to see her response to his touch. She froze, but only momentarily. Then he heard the slightest moan and he pressed his fingers deeper into her flesh, finding the small knots of tight muscle which revealed the tension she always carried. She tried to hide it but he knew her well.

As his thumbs probed her tense muscles, his fingers swept around her shoulders, stroking and caressing. She relaxed under his hands and leaned against him.

He kissed the side of her neck and, dredging up all his willpower, he stood up straight again. He couldn't risk losing himself in his feelings of lust.

He turned her in his arms.

"How are you feeling?"

"Tired." She cocked her head to one side and looked up at him with the sweetest of expressions. It nearly undid his intentions.

"So… you wish to go to bed."

She smiled, revealing the small dimples either side of her mouth. "I do."

He took a deep breath. He needed to be clear. "To sleep?"

Her lips twitched and she ran her hand up the lapel of his jacket, pulling back the cloth in a little tug, curling it around her hand. Her gaze roved up and down his face before settling on his eyes. She shook her head slightly. "No, Daidan. I want you to make love to me. Just as you used to." She sighed. "Close your eyes."

He narrowed them instead. "Why?"

She smiled. "So suspicious." She brushed a finger over his eyes and trailed it down his cheek, touching his lips before dropping her hand to her side. "Close them," she repeated.

With the memory of her finger upon his skin, he did as he was told.

"Do you remember when we first met?"

He closed his eyes more tightly as he recalled that evening. "Of course. I'd only just arrived in Helsinki from Australia to meet your father and I ended up meeting you first. I'd never been anywhere like this and was sitting in the park in the bright light of evening, overlooking the harbor, and then I saw you. You were wearing jeans and a t-shirt and were sitting alone also, listening to the music."

"And I looked over and caught you staring at me."

"Of course I was staring at you. I'd never seen anyone as beautiful as you. But it was something more. There was a quality that got to me. Somehow you managed to avoid all my defenses."

"And then you came and sat down beside me. Tell me what happened next."

He frowned. "Why? You know what happened as well as I do. It's almost as if you're needing some kind of reassurance. Do you?"

She shook her head in denial a fraction too late and he knew, for some reason, she was nervous.

"Tell me the truth."

She closed her eyes, exhaled a tightly held breath and

looked away. "You're right. I do feel kind of nervous. Stupid really."

He shrugged. "There's nothing to be nervous about. But Taina, we don't have to make love tonight, or tomorrow. We can wait until you're ready. There's no hurry."

As soon as he'd finished speaking her face relaxed. She had been scared.

"Come," he continued. "Let's go into the lounge, I'll pour you a drink and we can talk about whatever you like. About how we first met, about anything you like."

She nodded gratefully. "I'd like that."

He led her into the lounge and she walked to the windows and looked out over the sweep of harbor, dotted with lights. "Champagne?"

"That would be lovely."

By the time he'd returned, she'd kicked off her shoes and had her feet curled under her, on the sofa. He handed her the glass. "How about a toast?"

"What shall we drink to?"

"To us. And to taking things slowly." He held her gaze as they clinked glasses and took a sip. "Now." He placed the glass on the table and sat down beside her. "What shall we talk about?"

"Us. That first night."

"As I remember, I took you to my hotel and we made love."

"Is that all you remember?"

"You can't expect me to remember all our conversations."

"I guess not." She grinned. "Just the important bits."

But he wasn't smiling now. "They weren't the important bits. The important bits were that we were just two people. There was no money, no business, no families to come between us. No complications. Just us."

"Just us. Not for long though, was it?"

"No. We only had a few nights before I discovered you were the boss's daughter."

"And then everything changed." They were silent for a few moments.

"I know you don't believe me, but when I asked you to marry me the first time, my proposal had nothing to do with your father or the business. All the arrangements we made came later." He shrugged. "But those arrangements seemed normal to me—such marriages are a part of my culture."

"But not mine."

"No. Not yours."

"And nor is hitting someone flat to the ground who flirts with your girlfriend."

He bristled. "I was merely protecting you. That's what a boyfriend, a husband does."

"It nearly landed you in jail though, didn't it?"

He nodded briefly.

"You can't do anything like that ever again. You know that, don't you? The police warned—"

"I know what they warned. You don't need to tell me where my hot-headed passions can lead me. I know well enough. That's why they're contained. That's why I didn't follow you as I should have done."

She leaned back on the sofa. "I'm sorry. I wanted us to remember the good times. Do you think... that we could turn the clocks back, just for tonight? Just you, just me, just two people, before everything became so complicated?"

"Just two people," he repeated. "Of course."

He took her by the hand and they walked into the bedroom, barely aware of their surroundings.

Once inside he closed the door and kissed her. He'd meant it to be a gentle kiss to begin with but the nervousness she'd been showing earlier had now completely disappeared. And she turned the kiss into a totally sensuous experience—of lips upon lips, mouth opening onto mouth and tongue sweeping against tongue. As their kiss deepened he moved his hands over her shoulders, caressing the edges of her backless dress, skimming his thumb down, below the low rise of the dress. His fingers sought out the lacy strap of her underwear and he groaned, pulling her harder to him so she was left in no doubt as to how much he desired her.

He felt her gasp against his mouth and her hands roved under his jacket and then up inside his shirt. The feel of her hands against his bare skin was enough to drive nearly everything out of his mind. Nearly but not quite. Tonight was too important to him to mess it up by taking her as fiercely as he wanted to. He wanted to coax her, he wanted to enjoy her, but more than that he wanted her to want him as much as he wanted her. He wanted to make sure that she never left him again.

Reluctantly he pulled away from her mouth. He smiled as she leaned in to him, wanting more. Instead he brushed her cheek with his lips, pushed her hair back, nibbled her ear before moving lower. He remembered well the places on her body where he could arouse her with a single touch. But he wasn't leaving it to a single touch tonight.

He kissed the dip above her collar bone and was rewarded with an instinctive arching of her upper body, allowing him greater access, while her hips stayed pressed against his. He smiled to himself as he flicked his tongue into the same dip. She gasped and he kissed it harder, almost suckling the sensitive area. Their bodies just fitted together. Like some kind of elastic memory—their muscles and joints melded together as if they were one. And they would be soon.

He picked her up in his arms and walked over to the chaise at the foot of the bed. He untied the halter top which would have fallen to her waist if she hadn't crossed her arms against her breasts.

"I want to see you, Taina." He brushed his hands along her arms, willing her relax. There was no way he was going to force anything.

She bit her lip and nodded and let the dress drop to expose her breasts but still she held the dress tight against her stomach. Her breasts were small and round, their nipples hard and erect, waiting for his mouth.

"Perfect," he murmured. He lifted her to standing on the chaise, giving him more freedom to touch all of her. He licked around her nipple before taking it in his mouth and suckling it until it elongated.

Her hands swept into his hair, holding him where she wanted him to be. And he feasted on her—every part of his body, every thought and feeling was attuned to hers. He'd forgotten how good she tasted, forgotten how much he needed her. It was as if he'd been merely existing up till now —a man dying in the desert, who'd forgotten how good it was to have his thirst quenched. He moved to the other breast and felt the quickening of breathing as she responded like she'd always done.

He pulled away. "Taina," he murmured against her skin that smelled of peaches and cream. "God I've missed you."

He went to push down her dress but she stopped him and he looked up, surprised.

Although her breathing was still coming hard she clutched her dress to her stomach and there was something in her eyes that made him stop. Something he'd have described as fear if he'd thought it were a possibility.

"What's wrong? Am I going too fast?"

"No, nothing's wrong," she whispered. Then she sucked in a deep breath, shrugged and slipped off the couch and walked toward the door. He stood and watched, incredulous.

Was she just going to walk away? Then she stopped and turned off the light switch and darkness sank into the room. The only lights now came from the glow of the city that lay beyond the window. There were no neon lights to ruin the atmosphere, just the lights from the harbor and buildings around them.

"There," she said. "That's better."

"Whatever you want, Taina."

She took a few steps and paused. In the dim light he saw her pull the dress over her head in one swift movement and it fell to the floor. Now she was wearing only her black Louboutin heels and a white lacy thong. He didn't think he'd ever seen a sight more enticing. The shadows fell over her creamy skin revealing no detail but a sensual play of light and dark.

"So perfect." He held out his hand for her and she walked toward him, pushing her fingers through his. He gripped them and brought their joined hands to his lips. "Taina, you are so beautiful. I'd forgotten just how beautiful, how perfect you are."

Suddenly she pulled her hand away. "No one is perfect, Daidan."

"You are. Come here." He pulled her to him and kissed her again, intent on getting her to understand in no uncertain terms just how beautiful she was.

TAINA FELT MORE comfortable now it was dark. It had been so long since she'd been with Daidan. She couldn't bear to be a disappointment to him. All thoughts were swept away by his searching kiss and his equally searching hands, caressing her back, her bottom, slipping his hands under her brief thong, pulling it slightly so that it pulled against her clitoris. She gasped and pulled away.

His eyes narrowed, questioningly. She smiled and ran her hand up his shirt and pushed them both under his jacket. "You're wearing too many clothes."

He grinned and slipped out of his jacket. "This better?"

She shook her head.

He loosened his tie but got stuck on the knot.

She loosened it for him, pulling it from around his collar with a snap before tossing it to one side. Then she unbuttoned his shirt slowly until it hung loose, and placed her palms against his dark nutmeg skin—smoothly muscled and strong. She'd forgotten how it made her feel. How the brush of her hands against his skin made her feel deep inside, increasing her need for him.

She pressed her lips to his chest and then lower to his stomach. He held her there for a moment before pulling her away. He shrugged off his shirt while her hands shook as they tried to unzip his straining trousers. Her hands went to explore him further but he pulled her to standing.

"Not tonight, habibti. Tonight I want to see you. Tonight I want to make love to you, face to face, so that I can truly believe you are in my arms again."

He took her by the hand and led her to the bed.

CHAPTER 3

*T*aina fell back onto the silk sheets. Daidan knelt on the bed, his hands sweeping up her legs and pushing them apart. Then he took her foot and kissed it, caressing it with his mouth, massaging it with his fingers until she was writhing, desperate for him to be inside her.

And then he kissed her—not on the foot, not the knee not the thigh, but on her sex. His tongue probing the wetness he found there before licking that most sensitive area that throbbed with need. She gripped the sheets with her fists and began to pant, the ripples of orgasm instantly mounting, demanding release. He'd always been able to bring her to instant arousal with a few deft touches of his hands and tongue. And it was no different now.

"Daidan," she pleaded. But still he kept on with his wicked tongue and his fingers. Then suddenly he pulled away and in one swift movement had pushed deep inside of her with his cock. She came instantly. He stayed, buried deep within her as she cried out, her body shaking as wave after wave of release came over her.

He held her until it had passed and then he pulled out and

thrust deeply inside her again. He entwined his hands with hers and pushed them above her head. Between his hands and his hips she couldn't move even if she'd wanted to. He kissed her before pulling away too soon. She lifted her face to his but he shook his head, as he moved in and out of her in a slow, relentless rhythm which was already building up the coiling sensations inside her. Like the crackling electricity in the atmosphere before a storm, every part of her felt alive, more alive than she'd felt all the time she'd been away from him. And then she felt him tense and he grunted as his hips thrust deeply into her with deliberate strokes as he came into her. Her body orgasmed around him, drawing his seed deep into her body where she needed it. She lay back, eyes closed, pinned down by his arms, as slowly her breathing and body returned to normal.

She lay back, eyes closed, pinned down by his arms, as slowly her breathing and body returned to normal.

He kissed her mouth, her eyes and then rolled over her, pulling her against his side, into his arms. He stroked and kissed her hair. "*Habibti…*"

How had she managed to keep away from this devastating man for so long? He lay back, looking up at the ceiling as his hands caressed her body. She had her cheek to his chest and looked out to the dark night, stars punching through the dark mantle of the night. Same stars, same world as the Caribbean, but there was only one place for her… here, with this man. She needed him so much. But would he want her when he knew the truth?

"*Habibti,*" he whispered again, hugging her with his arm, tracing her skin with his other hand, for all the world like she was a treasure to him. And she knew that was how he'd always thought of her—a perfect prize, a treasure to be cherished. Except she wasn't that perfect prize, was she?

She pushed away the idea, not wanting the shrouds of

doubt to mar this moment. Not wanting any tears to fall from her eyes, down her cheek and touch his mahogany skin. She brushed her cheek against his body and they lay, neither wanting to talk, neither knowing what to say in that moment when bodily they were so close, but yet they were both so distant, full of doubts about the past, and fears for the future that not even this physical intimacy could overcome.

Slowly the stars shifted across the sky and the pattern of lights in the buildings changed and Daidan's breathing grew regular. His stroking of her arm ceased but his other arm continued to hold her firmly to his side.

SHE MUST HAVE FALLEN asleep at some point but she awoke before Daidan. There was a change in the sky. A glance at the clock showed her it was nearly 5:30. Daidan was always an early riser. She had to get up now, before it became too late.

She slipped out from under his arm and walked quietly to the bathroom. Her dressing room was through the opposite bathroom door and after showering she went there and dressed. She considered going back to bed but any sense of tiredness had left her. Instead she wandered into the lounge and opened the design folder which had been left for her and began looking through the jewelry designs.

SHE'D BECOME SO ABSORBED that she didn't notice the time moving on. It was only when she heard a "good morning," that she turned to see Daidan leaning against the wall with a cup of coffee in his hands.

"Daidan!"

He smiled. "You're surprised to see me?"

"No, of course not, it's just…" She shrugged. "I was absorbed in my work." He frowned slightly. She wasn't surprised. His tone had been warm toward her. Hers was more diffident, more tentative. She couldn't hide the fact that, despite the intimacy, something wasn't right. She couldn't hide the fact she felt on edge.

He placed the coffee on a table and walked to her and looked over her shoulder. He looped her hair behind her ear so he could see the design she'd been penciling. "You're working already?"

She doodled. "There's so much to do."

"So it's just as well I'm leaving today to go north, to the mine."

"You're going away?"

He nodded and rested against the wall, watching her with eyes that saw everything. "Just for a few days. I have some pre-arranged business I can't get out of but it'll give you time to work with the designers. Time to go The Warehouse and mock up some potential settings and see the stones. Get to know the new design team better."

She nodded. She might meet with the design team but there was no way on God's earth that she'd be going to her mother's design studio in The Warehouse. "Sure, I'll meet with the team. We'll be ready for your return."

"Good." He moved away. "Now, *habibti*, why don't you work from the apartment this morning? You look tired and I'll see you in a few days." His eyes darkened with desire once more. "And we will make love."

She rose and went to him. "I'd like that."

"Because you want a child."

"Not just that. I've missed you, Daidan. I've missed… us, together."

He nodded slowly. "Of course. We are meant for each other. And when I return I will show you again, how good we are together." He kissed her lightly despite the lust in his eyes. "I must go now. And don't forget to make arrangements for getting the Kielo necklace from the vault. I'd have done it but as you own it, the bank requires your approval."

Taina watched him leave the apartment. Then she moved to the window where, far below, his car rolled up to the entrance and the driver got out and opened the door for him. Meant for each other? Maybe once. But now? That depended on how Daidan reacted to certain facts which she simply couldn't risk telling him but that, she knew, he would inevitably discover. He'd find out, for sure. And then would he still want her?

～

"THE WAREHOUSE," Daidan instructed his driver upon returning to Helsinki.

"Your wife isn't there, sir."

Daidan frowned. "Where is she then?"

"In her office, in the city."

A thought suddenly occurred to him. "Has she been to The Warehouse at all?"

Their gaze met in the rear vision window. "Not to my knowledge, sir."

Daidan grunted. He'd given Taina instructions that she should work at The Warehouse. That was her end of the bargain. Seemed she'd not kept it. "Okay, the office, then."

As soon as he arrived he went to his office where he'd been told she was working. She was alone. She looked up and he was pleased to see her face flush with pleasure. It was all he could do to stop himself from going to her and taking her into his arms. But first he needed to know why she hadn't been to The Warehouse.

"Taina." He walked up to her. She rose and they kissed.

"How were your meetings?"

"Successful. As planned."

She grinned. "Of course they would be. You don't leave anything to chance, do you?"

The smile on his face froze. "No, not anymore." He didn't elaborate. He knew she wouldn't want to hear that he never intended to lose her again. He'd be accused of being too protective, too controlling. It was true, but there was no way he was going to change. "So, how did the past few days go?"

"Very well. I've done these." She twisted the design concepts around so he could see.

"They look good." He didn't take his eyes off her. "And the design team? You've been to The Warehouse to see them, of course?" He wanted to hear the truth from her. She shifted the papers on the desk to buy time. He could read her like a book and he didn't like what he was reading at this moment.

"No, I haven't been to The Warehouse." She shrugged. "There was no need."

"But you've retrieved the pieces which will make up the centerpiece of the collection?"

She shook her head.

"Why not? We need them. We need the Kielo necklace especially. You wore it for our wedding and took it with you when you left me. Presumably it's safely in your bank vault?"

She shook her head again and he tensed.

"Where is it, Taina?"

"I don't have it."

"That's not what I asked."

She looked at the desk as she gathered her papers together. "I don't know."

He wanted to grip her shoulders, to shake her, to kiss her, to do anything that would make her react to him. Instead he stepped away from her and clenched his fists. "What do you mean, you don't know?"

"It's none of your business. My father gave it to me when he knew he was dying. He'd always wanted me to wear that piece on our wedding day. It was mine to do with as I wished. Mine to give away if I wished."

"You gave it away?" He asked the question not truly believing she had.

She began to walk toward the door. "As I say, it's none of your business."

"It's *all* about business."

"Yes, of course it is. The lovemaking? Business. Wasn't it, Daidan? Are you using me again? Is that why you want the Kielo necklace so much? Ownership? Business?"

He ground his teeth, not daring to open his mouth and tell her the truth. It *was* about business. But there was no way he could show he didn't care for her. Not when he felt her in every nerve cell in his body, in every breath he took. She so consumed him that he didn't know *what* he felt any more.

"So... you won't tell me where the necklace is?"

"No." She smiled that polite cocktail-party smile she seemed to have developed since she'd been away.

Her distance fired his anger. He took a step closer and was rewarded with a flicker of something that briefly cracked her façade, like the ripple of heat across a desert, a mirage revealing an image otherwise hidden. It didn't matter which was the real Taina—it was enough to see the dichotomy, the confusion that lay beneath that pristine exterior. "You would never have lost something that was so precious to you. You've given it to someone. Who, I wonder?"

She bit her lip and he could see that he was on the right track. Or the wrong track. Because the thought that he'd stumbled on the truth made his heart sink.

"You won't tell me, hey? And why's that? Do you think I'm going to beat a path to the door of the lover you gave it to and pick a fight with him? Risk my reputation, my business, everything I've worked for?"

"It wouldn't be the first time."

There! It was confirmed. She'd given the priceless necklace to a lover. How could he have been so stupid? So dumb as to allow her into his bed, treat her like the woman he'd loved, and all the time she'd been deceiving him. But he refused to be the man she imagined him still to be—jealous and controlling.

"I'm not the same man I was before."

"Not jealous anymore? I can hardly believe that."

"I didn't say I'm no longer a man capable of jealousy. Merely that I have to be in love to be jealous." He saw the effect of his words on her face. That was fine with him. He wanted to hurt her as much as she was hurting him. The flare of anger in her eyes, followed by the upward tilt of her perfect chin. "If you really don't have the necklace, then you've simply made yourself more work. We need a centerpiece for the Northern Lights Collection. The design of that necklace informed and inspired all of your mother's work. It was the key piece. You and the designers are going to have to come up with a new focal point for the collection."

"And you expect me to do that in the time available?"

"Yes. You have the resources and you've inherited your mother's design skills—"

"Ha! I went straight from design college to marriage. I've *nothing* to show for my so-called design skills."

"I remember the design portfolio you produced—it was sensational. Just pick up where you left off. And you have a team of designers at your disposal to work with. Between you all you can do it. So make it happen."

"The launch is only months away."

"Taina, if you hadn't given away the Kielo necklace to some lover, or lost it, or whatever happened, you wouldn't have this problem. As it is, you *do* have the problem. Because like it or not, the launch is fixed for July at our castle. There will be fifty VIPs from around the world coming to our island home. And, if you haven't understood it yet, it's very important for the future of the company. It'll establish us at the forefront of the diamond industry. Your family connections are vital for this, vital for the brand."

"I'm just a 'brand' to you, aren't I?"

"No, you're not." She looked at him with eyes so wide and clear of obfuscation for once, that it nearly undid him. But there was too much confusion raging within him for it to be cleared with one look of her violet eyes. "No, you're more than a brand. If you still want me to keep my end of the bargain, you'll continue to be my lover."

He hated seeing the look of shock enter her eyes, as she turned away. "Of course. I'll keep my end of the bargain and you keep yours."

"It's what you wanted."

She glanced up, defensive. "It still *is* what I want."

"And how do you propose to do this if we can't even speak without arguing, without bitter recriminations? Had you thought of that? Or doesn't it matter to you? Are you so accustomed to sleeping with people you don't particularly like?"

Her face flushed with anger. "How dare you?"

He shrugged and leaned against his desk, as if he hadn't a care in the world. "I'm merely drawing a logical conclusion from what you've told me."

"It wasn't like that."

He shrugged again and pushed himself off the table and walked over to her. "So you keep saying and yet you won't tell me what it *was* like." He held her angry and confused gaze for a few seconds and then stepped away.

She drew the bundle of papers tight against her chest. "I'll be going then."

"To The Warehouse?"

"No. I've no time."

"Tomorrow then. You must go tomorrow. You must start on this. Time is running out."

TAINA PACED across the penthouse apartment once more. She'd been alone all evening. She'd dined alone and watched the lights of Helsinki from the top floor apartment shimmer and change as the evening progressed. And as each moment passed the tension inside her increased.

A few nights ago the lovemaking had been magical. She'd never allowed herself to imagine it would be so good. But she'd seen the change come over Daidan when she told him about the necklace.

Then she heard the elevator door open. Daidan walked into the main room, glanced at her and walked straight up to the cocktail cabinet and poured himself a whiskey. "You surprise me, Taina."

"Do I?"

He turned to her and took a drink from the tumbler. "You're still here."

"I've been here all evening. I was expecting you to return for dinner."

"I haven't eaten in the apartment for a long time."

"That's what the housekeeper told me before she left for the night."

He walked over to the desk and sifted through his mail. "What else did she tell you?"

"That she's worried about you."

He raised an eyebrow. "Really," he said dryly. "How nice that someone's worried about me."

"Yes. Seems you've unwittingly charmed someone into caring for you."

He grunted.

"Would you like anything to eat?"

"No. I ate out. Just as I eat out every night. Just as I intend to continue eating out." He walked over to her. "I don't fool myself that you've returned because you've a desire to be in my company. At least not out of the bedroom."

"And that's what you've come back for now?"

He smiled. Or at least the lift in his lips indicated it was a smile. But there was nothing in his eyes which looked the least bit amused. He looked hard, predatory almost. A shiver ran down her spine.

"Yes, that's exactly why I've come back. No need for me to go to any late night clubs, is there, not with my beautiful wife wanting me in her bed?"

"You usually go to clubs?"

"Sometimes. I've always had a strong sexual appetite. Or have you forgotten?"

She suddenly felt breathless and delicious shivers snaked their way down into her belly... and lower. She shook her head. "No, I remember."

He swilled his whiskey around his glass thoughtfully and then looked up at her with dark, dangerous eyes. "Tell me what you remember."

"Why?"

"I want to hear it. I want to hear what it is you remember of me. Tell me."

"I remember how you looked at me when you wanted me."

"A look. You remember a look. Must have been some look. Do I look like that now?"

"No. Then you looked at me as you wanted to make love to me, to savor me. Now, you look like you want to devour me."

He gave a brief laugh and set down his empty whiskey

glass. "Devour..." He turned suddenly to her. "That's quite a sexy word in itself." He came up to her, leaned into her and said it again. "Devour." His heated breath caressed her neck. She gasped and closed her eyes as her skin reacted to his warmth, raising her skin in a goose-bumped trail down her neck and across her chest. She clasped the sideboard behind her and wished she hadn't worn the silky dress without a bra, as she felt her nipples peak with desire.

She watched his gaze trail downward, watched the rapid rise and fall of her chest and her nipples become visible through the fine material. He rolled his head to one side and looked up at her lazily. He knew he had her for the taking. His hands remained in his pockets. He didn't attempt to touch her. "So my darling wife. I'd look at you. What else would I do?"

She swallowed and his gaze flitted down to her neck and then back up to her eyes. His eyes were narrowed and hooded, still the look of a predator. She might be the prey but she knew damn well, she'd be a willing prey to anything he wanted to do to her.

She licked her lips and again his eyes dropped momentarily to her lips. "You'd touch me," she half-whispered.

"I'd what?"

He'd heard. She knew he'd heard but he was using his control to force her to repeat herself.

"You'd *touch* me."

He raised his eyebrow and shook his head quizzically. "As in shake your hand, maybe?"

She shook her head. "You used to sweep your finger along my neck and tilt my chin up."

He withdrew his hand from his pocket and hovered his finger over her chest. She refused to show weakness and didn't move. She simply nodded. And then she felt it. She closed her eyes against the feel of his finger resting on her pulse point, her heartbeat racing. Then slowly he dragged one finger up her neck and tilted her chin up until her face was lifted close to his.

"Open your eyes, Taina." His voice was hoarser now—gruff, commanding.

She opened them and felt a stab of pure lust deep inside her at seeing his dark eyes so close to hers and his lips only a breath away.

"And then what did I do?"

"You kissed me."

He swayed close and then stopped. "Kissed you. My mouth against yours. My tongue finding yours, sliding against you, probing you just as you want to be probed deep inside. Because you did, didn't you Taina? You always wanted me inside you, filling you, straight away. You didn't want foreplay, did you? Not until after you'd been satisfied. Only then could I take my time with you."

How did she suddenly get so close to him? How come she hadn't noticed his other hand sliding around her back and bringing her hard against his body, against his erection, pressed against her belly? Because she was so damned turned on that all she could think about was the pulsing and swelling of her sex, the dampness accumulating between her legs.

"You didn't want foreplay, did you, Taina?" He demanded an answer while at the same time she shifted her hips against his. She couldn't stop herself.

She shook her head.

"I bet if I put my hand under that beautiful dress, if I stroked up your thigh, I'd find you wet for me. Wouldn't I?"

Her heart was beating like a drum, the pulse pounding in her head, drowning out everything except his mesmerizing voice. She shifted her stomach against him, opened her legs slightly and he pushed his hard thigh between them. She pressed her clitoris against his thigh and moved herself slightly, so slightly he surely wouldn't notice, and shifted her head to one side.

"Wouldn't I, Taina?" he demanded.

"Yes," she panted, hardly daring to move.

Then it happened. His mouth found her neck as his hand scooped up her dress and firmly rode up high along her inner thigh. He felt along the lacy edge of her thong before running his finger from back to front where she was soaking for him. With a grunt he gripped the fragile thong and pulled it away. She gasped as the back cut into her skin before the delicate silk gave away under his grip and his palm cupped her sex, his finger moving up and down along her wet folds.

She moaned as she leaned against him, moving her cheek against the fine material of his jacket. He held her firmly against him, while he stroked and caressed her intimately. She used to dream of him doing this, every night that they'd been apart. She'd awake wet and moaning, having dreamed that he'd made love to her but that was nothing compared to the reality of his touch. The tension grew in her body with each flick and slide of his fingers, nearly entering her but not quite. She pressed against his hand, grinding her clitoris into the heel of his hand, forgetting everything—including why she'd ever left this man whose body was so in tune with hers. She teetered on the edge of release and then, as if sensing how close she was, he thrust his fingers inside her and she came, with a loud shuddering climax.

She fell against him but he drew away. "You are as delicious as ever, my wife."

She lifted her head, awaiting his kiss but it didn't come. "Daidan, let's go to the bedroom."

He shook his head. "No. I want you here. With the lights of the city all around us."

He pushed her dress up and caressed her bare bottom.

She reached out for him then. "Hold me, Daidan. Hold me like you used to."

But he shook his head. "I can't do that, Taina. I don't know if I'll ever be able to do that because nothing's like it used to be."

And in that moment she realized how much not knowing what she'd been doing or who she'd been seeing, was tearing him apart. Behind that hard exterior, he was a man of passion, a jealous man and no doubt unable to rid himself of the notion that she'd given the precious necklace to a lover.

She gulped back her sadness. "Then do what you can."

He shrugged off his jacket. She came to him and unzipped his trousers, sweeping open his shirt, her hands brushing over his strong dark body. All he had on was his open shirt and the tie that still dangled carelessly. He looked at her hard and hurt at the same time as he dragged her dress up to her hips. Then he turned her around, bent her over the settee and came into her from behind.

He thrust into her, taking her with a devastating rhythm which made her cry out before he was ready. She gripped onto the edge of the settee as he continued to thrust into her, his rhythm quickening and he came inside her, shooting his seed deep into her body with a grunt. He pulled out of her and brought her to a standing position, his hands loosely around her waist. "Is that what you wanted, Taina?" he whispered in a devastating imitation of tenderness.

She refused to cry. She couldn't help but be turned on by him, still. But it had nothing to do with her need for an emotional connection with him.

"Is it?" he repeated. She nodded her head and then dragged off the sofa throw and pulled it around her and walked into the bedroom and locked the door.

CHAPTER 4

*T*aina awoke at the same time she'd awoken each of
the past ten mornings since that fight and did the
same thing—lay there alone in the enormous bed and
listened. But she listened in vain because there was no sound.

She propped herself up on the white and coffee-colored
pillows and looked blankly out the uncurtained window. She
didn't recognize the sweeping harbor that spread before her,
veiled in that curious half-light of pre-dawn. It would be that
way for a few more hours yet. She'd forgotten the beauty of
light that was not light. And she'd forgotten what it was like
to be alone. She'd made sure she'd never been alone in the
year she'd been away. And she'd paid the cost.

She rose, unhooked her ivory silk robe from the chair
and, tying it around her, walked over to the floor-to-ceiling
triple-glazed windows of the inner city apartment. The
awakening lights of Helsinki spread below her like a jeweled
veil. It was still mostly dark at that hour even though it was
now May and the first signs of summer were appearing—
usually a reason for celebration, but not for her, not now.

She hadn't seen Daidan since that night when they'd had

47

sex—there was no way she could call it making love—after which he'd disappeared into thin air. He hadn't come to bed and he must have left the apartment in the small amount of time she'd managed to sleep. He'd been gone by the time she'd reached the office. The official line was that he'd been called suddenly to Amsterdam on business.

He'd left her no note, no email, nothing to explain his sudden absence. She was sure it was in response to what had happened because his staff appeared equally surprised.

Did he hate her so much because she'd given away the necklace? Did the fact that she was so ready for him despite the fact he believed she'd had an affair, so turned on by him, disgust him? Whatever the reason it was obvious that he regretted his part of the bargain. He didn't want to be anywhere near her.

She walked into the bathroom and turned on the shower as she looked at herself in the mirror. At least he could get away, she thought bitterly. She had to live with the self-hate. She turned away from her reflection not wanting to see herself, so perfect, so blond, so beautiful—and so ugly inside. That's what she did, wasn't it? Turned love into something negative. It was her curse.

She opened her robe and looked at her body under the harsh bathroom light. It was good that she'd insisted that the lights be turned down, that he hadn't seen her. He hadn't understood but it was better that he didn't know. Not yet.

Then she let her hands drift down to her sex and she pressed against it and closed her eyes, imagining Daidan's hands against her body as they were ten nights before. Her senses were still heightened by the sex and by her own emotional needs which the lovemaking had stirred, despite the intervening days.

Daidan hadn't kissed her and he'd not caressed her other

than intimately. He'd given her what she'd asked for and nothing more. Did she want more? She opened her eyes.

She hadn't looked beyond a child, beyond the sex act, when she'd decided to return. She'd thought they could have the kind of family life her parents had had—distant but functional—at least it had been in the beginning. She hadn't imagined it would be this hard, having him physically but not having him emotionally.

Did she want more?

She turned her back on the mirror and stepped into the shower, refusing to acknowledge the truth she saw in her eyes. She'd always refused to want more than she could have. Up till now.

TWO DAYS later Daidan flew into Helsinki airport. Despite the fact he'd only lived there a few years he felt it to be more a home to him than Ma'in, the country of his birth where, as middle son, he was neither the eldest son and heir, nor the charming youngest son. No, he had no wish to do any more than visit his home country. His place was out in the world, creating an identity for himself, on his own merits.

And that's what he'd done. From an early age he'd lived in colder climates. First in Switzerland where his mother used to take them skiing. There, he'd stayed on, insisting on attending a Swiss international school. Excelling at everything, he'd had his choice of universities and had chosen Harvard. After Harvard he'd gone to Australia, but only long enough to gain experience working in its biggest diamond extraction company. There he forged a life-long friendship with the owner, Amelia, with whom he'd had a brief affair before she'd married, before heading off to Finland to work for Taina's father.

His visit to Finland was only meant to have been of short duration to learn more about the industry he'd chosen to work in—diamonds. But then he'd met Taina. And now he couldn't conceive of living anywhere else. He'd fallen for Taina the first day he'd seen her. Yes, he'd wanted the diamond company, but he'd wanted Taina more. And that was his blessing and his curse.

HE WAS BACK in the country. She knew Daidan had been in touch with the office because the tension was palpable. But Taina continued to listen to her assistant running through the phone messages.

"And…" her assistant continued nervously. "We've received word from your husband. He's asked that you meet him in The Warehouse in an hour."

Taina continued to bring the glass of water to her lips. But she didn't drink, just looked out at sunlight on the beautiful neoclassical buildings of central Helsinki. It had been light since five a.m. It was only another couple of months before the launch. She and the other designers had a lot of work ahead of them but that wasn't what was concerning her now. Why was Daidan insisting she meet him in The Warehouse? What right did he have to demand her to drop her plans and go to The Warehouse?

She turned around and carefully placed the glass on the table. Iittala glass. Like everything else in this building—twentieth-century Finnish design, selected by her mother and now a collector's piece.

"Thank you." She glanced across to Daidan's office. She smiled. "Is everything prepared for this morning's meeting?"

"Yes but we thought as you'd be going to The Warehouse—"

"The meeting will continue as arranged. I'll hold it in my

husband's office. I want to be sure that all the details of the launch are covered."

"Yes, but…"

"No buts. The meeting will continue as arranged."

Daidan would have to learn, she thought as the door closed behind her assistant, that she might have returned, she might have struck a bargain with him, but she wasn't, and would never be again, a man's pawn for him to use as he liked.

TAINA SAT at the head of a pine table. The white overhead pendant lamps and other modernist details suited her, Daidan thought, even as he walked, unannounced into the room. Everyone, except Taina who was speaking, cast nervous glances toward him.

But he wasn't going to yell at her in front of their staff, as much as he might like to. He leaned back against the closed door and crossed his arms, listening as Taina continued without missing a beat.

"And the Paris branch of the Triple X Agency will look after all the details of our meeting there next week. But they'll need answers to print branding." She looked across to one of her team. "Pascal?"

"Sure. It's in hand. I'll contact them this morning."

"And Aarne, you've made all the arrangements for Paris? All the details covered?"

"Just need to book your return flights from Paris to Helsinki. I understand you won't be traveling to Ma'in?"

Taina frowned. "No. No, I won't." She turned to another person at the table. "And the main event? The opera in the castle?"

"Everything's been arranged. The guests have been invited."

She frowned. "Can you let me have the final copy, please."

The executive glanced nervously at Daidan. "Certainly."

"Let's just hope the weather improves by then," Taina commented wryly.

Daidan hadn't intended to stay. He'd walked into the meeting room angry that she'd disregarded his instructions. But, as he listened to her working with her staff, the anger dissipated. In the ten days he'd been absent she'd worked hard to get up to speed on a project which had been underway for six months. He'd anticipated that she would be merely a figurehead, only nominally in charge. Someone to front the campaign. He frowned. Looked like she was taking on more than he'd imagined. That wasn't what he'd planned. He'd thought she'd focus on the design aspect, not the overall plans.

He pushed himself off the wall. "Taina! A moment please."

He cast a frowning look at the others and they melted out of the room.

She rose from her seat, immaculate in a black roll-neck top and vintage loose trousers that sat on her hips, accentuating her slim frame. She was the picture of a cool wealthy executive. Apart from the set of her mouth and her narrowed eyes. She folded her arms and cocked her head to one side. "A moment? Just the one?"

He walked up to her and sat on the edge of the table. "That's what I said."

"It may have escaped your notice but I was in a meeting. You wanted me to work. I'm working. And yet you decide to interrupt my meeting, to flex your muscles by showing everyone that you're the boss, not me."

He raised an eyebrow. "I am the boss. However, it wasn't my intention to show everyone that because they know."

She grunted in frustration.

He shrugged carelessly and walked away, needing to get

away from her before he bridged the distance between them and hooked her head and kissed her. But that way led to madness. As had happened last time they were alone together. It had taken him days to recover. Ridiculous! He wouldn't let it happen again. "So why didn't you come to The Warehouse?"

She sat as if suddenly tired and pushed her hands through her hair, which immediately flopped back into place—the fringe of blond hair falling into perfect shape, framing her oval face, sweeping brows and large eyes. Desire snapped in his gut. He walked over to the window, willing the now bright light to neutralize his need for this woman—a need that he was scared would destroy him and everything he'd worked for.

"Because I had a meeting scheduled. You wanted me to work. I'm working. Okay?"

"You should have left it to the team. They're quite capable."

"I know that. But I'm doing what you asked me to do."

"I *asked* you to come to The Warehouse." He turned back to face her then. "To your mother's jewelry business. We need to discuss what we're going to show, examine the mock-ups, and figure out which pieces we'll make replicas of to take with us for the launches in the US and Europe. There's a lot to do." He shook his head. "You know, I don't understand you at all. You're a designer and yet you refuse to visit your mother's prestigious premises."

"I don't refuse. I just prefer not to be summoned."

"And I only summon you when you don't appear as needed." He narrowed his gaze. "It's almost as if you're scared of something."

She turned away quickly. "Why would I be scared of a building?"

"No idea. You tell me. Scared of old ghosts?"

She shook her head and rose, jutting out her jaw in a gesture he recognized. He'd stirred her stubborn streak. "You know? I don't think I'm scared of anything anymore. Let's go, shall we?" She strode out of his office to her desk where she grabbed her oversized bag from which beautiful designer contents spilled, and shrugged a loose wool jacket over her shoulders.

He narrowed his eyes as that flicker of need for her flared into life again as he followed her out into the open-plan office and waited for her by the elevator.

He'd extended his business to ten days hoping the time apart would help him get his feelings under control. But he'd badly underestimated them. He doubted ten months would be long enough. She walked past him on a wave of expensive perfume. Make that ten years...

DAIDAN SPENT the entire drive to The Warehouse on his phone, while Taina stared out the window watching central Helsinki pass by. They'd soon driven over the canal that separated the island of Katajanokka from the rest of the city and passed by Uspenski Cathedral, with its extravagant gold spires and red brick, on their way to the docks. Not far away was the quay where they kept their boat for trips to their island home, but they turned away from that and headed instead to one of the coolest and most expensive addresses in Helsinki—the old warehouses with an unsurpassed view of the harbor and its archipelago of small islands. The warehouse had been in Taina's family for generations but it had been her mother who'd supervised its conversion into a sought-after design studio.

They parked in front of the centuries old, beautiful brick building and Taina looked up at its soaring architecture, complete with extravagantly sized windows through which light streamed. It was beautiful, but Daidan had been right. She was scared of old ghosts. And not just her mother's.

Daidan stepped to one side and held the door open for her. He'd always been old-fashioned in his manners. It had been one of the things that she'd loved about him. But now it meant she had to enter the building first. She gritted her teeth and stepped in over the worn threshold. The smell of the place got her first. She almost thought she'd faint as the devastating combination of polished wood and lilies of the valley—the kielo—swamped her. Seems the staff of designers still maintained her mother's tradition of having lilies everywhere.

She looked around. Nothing much had changed which only made it harder. She pretended to be caught up in looking at a painting on the wall. Really she was just buying time. Daidan went up to the group of designers and began talking with them, leaving her to her own devices for a few vital minutes—minutes she needed to settle her nerves. She glanced anxiously at the stairs. She just hoped she'd be able to avoid climbing the polished staircase to her mother's own studio.

"Taina!" Daidan called. She walked over to him, her boots clicking on the worn parquet floor and greeted the team of designers, all of whom she'd been meeting with in the office tower. "Look." He showed her some drawings. "We still have these pieces. And Emilia has agreed to construct something similar to the Kielo necklace. And we have the paste replicas we can go with in the meantime." He nodded to the woman. "Thank you, Emilia."

He took Taina by the arm. "Come on, let's go upstairs."

Taina resisted. There was no way she was going up there.

"I'll stay here. There are a few things I want to discuss with the designers."

But Taina could see from Daidan's face that she wasn't going to get away with it.

"Upstairs, in your mother's old office. I'd like to talk with you there."

She didn't want to be dragged kicking and shouting upstairs by him, in front of everyone, so she did what he wanted. She could do this. So long as the rear door was closed.

He followed her up there and she breathed a sigh of relief. The partition wall was closed and the rear of the office—the part that still remained from the eighteenth-century warehouse that it once was—was sealed off. She immediately went and sat at the window seat that overlooked the wooded park outside. She suddenly realized it was the seat she'd always made a bee-line for as a youngster when she'd been allowed to visit her mother. Old habits died hard it seemed.

"Taina!" She jumped and twisted around. It was as if her father had come back to life.

Daidan was sitting behind her mother's desk—although in all truth her mother had never used it. It had been something her father had insisted she have. "You're the director of this company—you should act the part," he'd barked at her mother. Her nervous, elegant mother had simply shrugged it off and avoided the subject. Her father had got his way in installing the elements of the office, but her mother had never used the desk. And now Daidan sat there, just as her father had.

"It suits you," she said.

He frowned. "What does?"

"The desk." She rose and walked over to it, determined not to be undermined by Daidan. "Always wanting to command, eh Daidan?" She leaned against the rough brick wall, the soft wool of her long jacket catching on the rough stone.

"Someone has to, Taina. You've been gallivanting about God knows where, with God knows who for over a year."

"And don't you wish you knew!"

He shrugged. "I really couldn't care less."

"I don't believe you. I bet you've had me followed. I bet even now there are people trying to work out where I was last seen and with whom."

"Of course," he said in a bored tone. "But not for any sentimental reasons. I want to know who has the necklace. That's all."

"I should have known. Business. That's all you care about, isn't it?"

"Exactly. And if you'd tell me where it is, it would make all our lives that much easier."

She shook her head.

His eyes flashed and he walked over to her and stood too close. "How could you betray your mother like this? Giving away your family heirloom, something your grandfather found, your own mother created? Have you no feeling?"

"I have feelings all right and don't you dare claim I haven't."

"Where were your feelings when you left Antigua then? When I was away I discovered something new about you. One of the last times you were seen—only two months after you left me—was at a party after which you disappeared into thin air. Did you drink too much? Did you flirt and leave with some man?"

She shook her head as the memory of that night came back to her. "It wasn't like that."

"I know men, Taina. I know them. You left the party with someone. And then you disappeared. Off the face of the planet for the rest of the year."

She shook her head again. He was close. Too close for his own good. She had to divert him, make him angry, make him argue, make him do anything except guess the truth. Because she was scared that if he did that he'd react as he'd done in the past and lash out. Except this time the consequence wouldn't be simply a telling off by the police—it would mean his ruin.

"You hate it when something happens you can't control, don't you?" she said, purposely goading him.

He shook his head, grinding his teeth. "You never used to be so hard, Taina."

"And who do I have to thank for that? My father and you."

"You knew what you were getting in to. It was your world."

"The world I wanted to escape from. My father kept me a virtual prisoner on the island for years after my mother died, taught by a series of tutors. Even when I went to university I was escorted there and back by my father's secretary. I only left the island when either he allowed me to, or when he was away and I took the boat to the city myself. Like I did when I met you. It was only because he approved of you that I was allowed to see you again and I gained some measure of independence."

"Is that all I was? An excuse for you to escape? Maybe you changed your mind about being with me when you realized it was a world I didn't want to escape from?"

"There was so much I didn't know."

"How could you live in your family and not know?"

"Because I was bloody naïve. And you and my father took advantage of that. I was stuck on the island while this"—she cast her arms around the studio—"was the only place I ever thought about."

He frowned. "And yet you didn't want to come here now. Why?"

She made a mistake then and glanced toward the closed door. He saw the direction of her gaze and walked toward the door.

"Don't!"

"What?"

Suddenly one of the designers came up the stairs. "You wanted to see the lists and drawings?"

She spread them on the wooden trestle table that had been her mother's work table. Absently, Taina toed the groove in the wood that the stool had made when her mother sat there in her chosen position at the drawing board.

"Oh, we found a box of your mother's things. Just bits and pieces when we were clearing it out."

"Can I see?"

"Sure. We put them somewhere." He went and looked. "Yes, here they are."

Daidan and the man looked over the drawings while Taina returned to the window seat with the box. There were the initial drawings for the next range, lists and then, at the very bottom, a small sketch of Taina, knees pulled up to her chin, gazing out from the same window seat upon which she now sat.

She held it to her nose and smelled it, irrationally hoping for a residue of the scent of her mother's Chanel No 5, but of course there was none. It had been over ten years ago, after all. It was dated on the back—a week before her fourteenth birthday. Of all her birthdays, her fourteenth had been the worst and the one she remembered most clearly. It had been the day her father had told her that he and her mother were separating and that Taina had to choose—choose between living with her alcoholic mother or him. Taina had been in shock, not least because her family never discussed any 'unpleasantness', such as finding her mother passed out on the bathroom floor. It had always been dealt with in the same way—by ignoring it. Daidan had always described her as being "aloof" and no wonder—from any early age she'd learned to hide all her thoughts and feelings.

Taina slipped the sketch into her bag and rose. Only then did she see that the doors were opened. Inevitably her eyes were drawn to the hook that still hung there, from which goods had been hoisted in the olden days from the quay into the warehouse. The hook on which she'd found her mother hanging, dead for days.

She stifled a sob and turned and ran down the stairs and out of the building.

She jumped into the car but she wasn't quick enough and Daidan followed her.

"Are you going to tell me what the hell that was all about?"

She couldn't speak even if she wanted to. She was scared if she opened her mouth to speak, nothing but a wail would emerge.

He sat back grimly. "You have too many secrets, Taina. Too many and I *will* find them out."

Maybe some, she thought, as they pulled out into the traffic. But not all. Not if they were to have a future together.

CHAPTER 5

*T*he private jet joined the stack of planes that coiled above Paris, waiting for their descent into Charles de Gaulle airport.

Daidan looked up as the door to the bedroom opened but it was only an air steward. He sighed and turned back to the computer once more. Taina hadn't emerged from the bedroom at all on the flight and he'd stayed in the main cabin, working. Or so it would seem to everyone else, he thought as he tried to re-read an email for the tenth time.

In truth he'd been trying to figure out what the hell was going on with Taina. Part of him wanted to barge into the bedroom and force her to tell him. He grunted. Force? That was a laugh. The only time he'd ever resorted to violence was when some guy had kept pestering her before they'd married. He'd seen red and it had cost him dearly. One blow and the man had fallen back and hit his head and nearly died. Ever since then he could see that Taina was worried he'd lose his temper again and risk everything he'd worked for. But he wouldn't. He couldn't imagine the amount of rage that would be needed to take him over the edge. He only had one weak

61

spot, and that was Taina. And she was here, now, safe with him.

But she was hiding something. And he *would* find out. He just had to keep alert. She'd give herself away sooner or later and then he'd find his bearings and get them both on track once more.

The door opened suddenly and Taina stepped out, looking like every Parisian fashion designer's favorite muse. With her drop-dead good looks and flawless style that she'd become known for, the face of Kielo Diamonds would blast the competition out of the water.

"How are you, Taina?"

"Okay. Just a little nervous about the meetings."

"You'll be fine. Come, take a seat. We'll be landing in around five minutes."

She sat opposite him, clicking her belt into place. "We're going to La Société first?"

He nodded. "La Société Diamant is our most important potential client."

"Papa tried for years to work with them but they weren't interested."

"They wouldn't be interested now if we were on our own, but working with the Australian mine, we're big enough to make them pay attention. And carve a place for ourselves in the Antwerp and Mumbai markets. We couldn't have done it without Amelia. And Mark," he added. "Although I reckon she'd be better off without Mark from what I've heard."

Taina turned away suddenly and looked out of the window. "But they won't be at the meeting, will they?"

"No."

"Nor at the launch?"

"No. I told you. Taina? Is anything the matter?"

She gave him a quick tense glance and shook her head. "Of course not. What could there be?"

She'd gone from relaxed and interested, to tense and wary in a single moment. What had he said to create that change in her? Not La Société Diamant— she'd brought them up herself. Amelia maybe? "Did you catch up with Amelia while you were away?"

She shook her head. Did he imagine it or did her lips tremble slightly?

He touched her cheek with his finger and turned her to face him. "What is it?"

"Just a little nervous about today. I told you."

"Is that all?"

"Yes." The plane landed smoothly and Taina forced a smile. "So, all we have to do is show them that, while we may be small, we're a well-established, reliable family company and can supply a different type of cachet."

"Exactly." But Daidan didn't smile back. Instead he looked grimly out the window at the city that lay beneath them as he tried to figure out what in their conversation had really unnerved her because it wasn't the meetings—he sensed her excitement about those. He'd find out, sooner or later. But he knew it wouldn't be sooner. For now, they were both covering their true thoughts with superficial talk. He turned to her once more. "And with you on my side, I can't lose. There's only one thing the French love more than a beautiful woman."

She cocked her head to one side.

"And that's a stylish woman."

TURNED OUT DAIDAN WAS CORRECT. The meeting had gone well with the press anxious for shots of the foreign prince and the stylish Finn.

Taina snapped the paper open at another shot of them and passed it to Daidan who sat opposite her in the French café. June in Paris was entirely unlike June in Helsinki, she thought. As much as she adored her home city, the warmth of a summer's day in Paris was very seductive.

"See," she said, lifting her chin to the warmth of the summer sunshine. "Everything will be fine."

He downed a glass of water and shook his head. "You, Taina, could charm the birds from the trees. Monsieur Betrand is as grizzled a campaigner as they come and you had him eating out of the palm of your hand."

She laughed and replied without opening her eyes. "What can I say? It's a gift."

He didn't reply immediately and she opened her eyes to see his face serious and intense. She had no idea where his thoughts were leading and she didn't want to know. Her smile faltered.

"Anyway." She took a sip of her kir royale. "What made you choose this café? A little bohemian for you, isn't it?"

"I thought it would make a change. We've been surrounded with formality ever since you returned."

"So is that why you dismissed the driver?"

"Partly." He placed his elbows on the table and rested his chin on his steepled fingers. "You really don't remember?"

She looked away. She did. Of course she did. She just hadn't thought *he'd* remembered. She looked up from beneath lowered lashes. "Tallin?"

"Of course, Tallin. It was the only holiday—no matter how brief—we had in the year we dated before we got married. Your father always had me tied up with work. But in Tallin we had no chauffeurs, no itinerary, just walking, eating and…" The look in his eyes was positively indecent.

"Um, I remember. And you said next time, it would be Paris."

"I never imagined that next time would be a reunion of sorts."

"Reunion," she repeated thoughtfully. "I guess it is."

"You know, when I first saw you I thought, what a sweet girl."

She raised her eyebrows in surprise. "Sweet?"

"Yes, sweet. You were wearing a simple t-shirt and jeans."

"Must have been my rebellious college phase."

"And thank God for it." He glanced down at her hips. "I miss those jeans."

"I don't know where they are."

"I do. In your wardrobe on the island."

There was something about the fact that he knew where this old item of clothing was that touched her. He must have gone looking at some point. She cleared her throat.

"And you, I don't remember seeing you dressed in jeans for ages. Nor a shirt without a tie." She reached forward and playfully tugged his tie. "Maybe it's a part of you now. Clipped to your collar is it?"

He narrowed his eyes playfully. "*This*, I'll have you know is an Ermenegildo Zegna silk tie, picked up last time I was in New York."

She sat back in her seat suddenly. "When were you in New York?"

"Ten months ago." He paused and took another sip, then looked up at her with a keen glance. "On business. Before you left, you'd agreed to attend the charity ball in New York. I thought you'd be there. But you never showed up."

She waited for him to ask why she hadn't.

He shrugged. "So rather than come away empty-handed, I purchased an expensive tie." He reached over and took her hand. "I'm curious, of course I am, Taina, but you must have good reasons not to tell me so I'm not going to keep asking. Okay?"

She nodded. "So how about we have a date when we get

back? Both of us in our jeans. We could go to Storyville. Remember? That jazz place near the Parliament building?"

"How could I forget? Yes, I'd like that. Now drink up. It's a beautiful evening. Let's go for a walk along the Seine."

They weren't the only strollers out that evening. She slipped her arm through his and they walked along the river bank, below Quai de Montebello, past Notre Dame. Paris was at its best, with the low afternoon light warming the cream-gray limestone buildings. The flowers were in blossom and romance was in the air. They walked over the Pont de la Tournelle to the Île Saint-Louis, and along to the Place Vendôme and then to the Triangle d'Or looking in the various shop windows. Hours passed without notice. They were still discussing the jewelry they'd seen when the rain came. They ran, laughing, into a dark café basement, complete with individual booths and thudding music. Daidan ordered some wine.

He looked around. "I think you're right about those jeans. Next time I travel I'll bring them with me. I think we're the odd couple out here."

"Yes, this truly is bohemian. Like The Warehouse."

There was silence for a few moments. "What was your mother like? I know so little about her. Only that knowledge which is public."

"Public? Like the fact she was an alcoholic who died of a heart attack?"

"Yes." He shrugged. "Plus the history of her designs."

"Yes, well the design history would be accurate but not much else."

"You mean she wasn't an alcoholic?"

"Unfortunately she was that." She hesitated. But it was time he knew. "But she didn't die of a heart attack. That was something my father put about. Mustn't have the family name or business adversely affected by scandal."

"What kind of scandal?"

Taina took a sip of wine, wondering why she'd chosen now to tell Daidan. But she knew why. He'd offered her an olive branch and she'd enjoyed spending time with him. It was as if the past year hadn't happened. She couldn't tell him all her secrets and she prayed he'd never find out some of them, but this one she could. It would help him to understand her a little. "My mother committed suicide."

His eyes widened with surprise and he squeezed her hand. "Taina, I'm so sorry. That must have been terrible for you. How old were you?"

His immediate concern for her welfare warmed her. "I was fourteen—it happened ten years ago."

"How did it happen?"

"She hung herself. On the hook at the end of her studio."

"The hook? No wonder you didn't… But how did you know your father hushed it up?"

"I found her." Her voice faltered. Deciding to tell Daidan was one thing, but actually telling him was bringing the memories back with painful force. She sucked in a calming breath and glanced up, trying to suppress the tears. "In her studio. Hanging."

"Oh my God!"

"And it was my fault."

"Taina! You were fourteen. How can you possibly blame all this on yourself?"

"Because when I was fourteen my mother and father separated and my father made me choose between living with my mother or living with him. I was scared of my mother when she was drunk. And my father was so controlling that he was very hard to say 'no' to. So I said I'd go with him. I can still remember the look on my mother's face. She was devastated."

"You were fourteen! Your father should never have put you in that position."

"He did it because he knew I wouldn't be able to say 'no' to him. And he knew that it would shatter my mother and he wanted to hurt her. You see, she'd fallen in love with someone else."

"I'd always thought it was your father who'd left your mother because of her drinking."

"No. That was something he spread about. They just wanted to lead separate lives. Poor Mama didn't stand a chance with him as her enemy. That day I found her, I'd gone to tell her that I'd changed my mind and that I wanted to live with her. I'd gone to tell her that I loved her. But it was too late."

Daidan moved to sit beside her. He put his arm around her and she placed her cheek against his chest. "Christ, Taina, I never knew. We met when you were twenty-two, and I wondered why you seemed so withdrawn from your father."

"It was my only way of coping. Father didn't seem to think there was a need for me to have therapy so I just coped with it on my own. You were my therapy, Daidan. You."

"I had no idea." He paused. "Taina, why don't you come with me to Ma'in tomorrow?"

She sat back and looked at him with surprise. "Ma'in? Are you sure?"

"You've only ever met my brothers at our wedding. It's about time I took you to my homeland. Sahmir and his wife will be there."

"Sahmir? Married? Who'd have thought?" She laughed, remembering the charming Sahmir who'd flirted with her shamelessly.

"And who'd have thought we *wouldn't* be?" He paused. "I mean it, Taina. Why don't you come?"

"I don't understand why you'd want me to."

WANTED: A BABY BY THE SHEIKH

"Because you're my wife, maybe?"

"And is that really why you want me to come?"

"Partly. And also maybe because I'm tired of being the strange uncle whose wife deserted him. Maybe because I'd like to maintain a united front. Maybe because it'll give us a chance to talk business, uninterrupted, about the launch and the future of the company. And maybe…"

"Another maybe?"

"And… maybe… because I simply want your company."

She could have argued against all of those "maybes" except the last one. That one floored her.

"Look at us now. Away from your father's business legacy, away from the pain of your history, we're good together. And in the bedroom, I know we can be good together. We could make it work this time."

Inside her a voice screamed "no". There was still too much he didn't know. She nodded and heard herself agreeing. "I'd like that."

"Good."

"But…" She pressed her lips together as she tried not to smile. "The bedroom bit…"

He narrowed his eyes suspiciously. "Yes?"

"Tell me how you're so sure." She shrugged innocently. "Because we've only made love twice since I've returned and the last time was memorable for all the wrong reasons."

"Hm. The number of orgasms I gave you aren't good enough reasons to remember our lovemaking?"

She nearly choked on her drink as she looked around to see if they'd been overheard. But the music was so loud it seemed unlikely. And, she noticed, being at the back of the room, the walls of the booth kept them completely hidden from view. She shifted her leg closer to his and he put his hand on her thigh beneath the table. Her breath hitched and she moved her face closer to his, her lips brushing his chin, the rough stubble stimulating her even further. She moaned as his hand slid under her dress and moved up her inner thigh. She closed her eyes as he massaged her leg, his thumb tantalizingly brushing her sex every now and then. But his hand didn't move any higher.

"How about a little aperitif." He dipped his head to her ear and whispered. "An orgasm now to get you in the mood and then more later."

If he was expecting any kind of verbal response, he was out of luck. All Taina could think about was movement of his hand against her bare skin, suggestive and tempting and... driving her crazy. She kissed him, pressed closer to him, and hoped her movements would push his hand higher up her leg. It did.

As the kiss deepened, he fanned out his fingers in the narrow gap between her thighs until the side of his hand was pressed hard against her sex—covered only by the damp silk of her knickers. She hooked one thigh over his to allow his hand greater access and he took the hint. His hand immediately slid beneath her thong and played along the wet length of her lips, just as his tongue played in her mouth. She tipped her head back, her mouth open, allowing him to plunder her just as his fingers pushed deep inside her. She moved against him harder now, her clitoris ramming against the V of his thumb and forefinger as he pleasured her to within an inch of her life. Less than an inch. Because with a loud cry, only partly drowned by the thudding beat of the music, she felt she'd died and gone to heaven as she collapsed against him.

"My Taina. I adore pleasuring you. You melt under my touch. Like some delicious dessert that I need to taste. Come..." He straightened her dress. "Let's go to my family's home and I will make good my promise to you. Luckily there's no one else staying there at present."

Taina needed no further incentive and they'd soon hailed

a cab and were drawing up outside the Paris home of the royal family of Ma'in in the Place Des Vosges. She looked up at the impressive house as Daidan paid the cab driver.

She whistled. For all the wealth she was accustomed to, these mansions were something else with their smart brick and stone striped façade and vaulted arcade which fronted them, held aloft by pillars. "I didn't know your family had a house in Paris."

"There is so much you don't know, Taina."

Once out the taxi he took her hand and unlocked the house. Taina walked through the rooms, admiring the graceful proportions and the beautiful antique furniture.

"If this is only your *pied-a-terre* in Paris, I can't imagine what your family home is like."

"The palace in Ma'in? It's grand. Of course it's grand. My father made sure of that."

"How come you never talk about it?"

"Because it's my home no longer. I feel more at home in Helsinki than Ma'in."

"Really? Why, when you spent so much time in Ma'in?"

He shrugged as he poured them both a glass of champagne. "I didn't really spend so much time in Ma'in. As soon as I could, I left. Studied overseas. Worked overseas."

She accepted the glass and went to the window to look out at the gardens opposite, mysterious in the long twilight of a Parisian summer. She opened the window and leaned out. "Is that a fountain I can hear?"

"Yes. It's where Sahmir first met Rory."

"Really? How did that come about?"

"You'll have to ask her when you come to Ma'in. Because"—he said pulling her away from the window and into his arms—"I have more important things on my mind now." He brushed his lips against hers.

"Such as?" she murmured against his skin.

"I believe I promised you something."

"Some *thing*? Singular? I don't think so."

"Um, more than one. And I never renege on a promise. Always deliver in full."

"Now how many was it"—she laughed as he took her hand and they raced up the stairs—"six maybe, or was it more?"

He stopped and kissed her, their panting breath having little to do with the exertion. "As many as you wish, *habibti*," he murmured against her cheek as his hands wandered. "And as fast or as slow as you wish…"

A FEW HOURS later Daidan rolled off Taina and lay panting, on his back. "I should have known you'd choose 'fast'. You, my darling, are an impatient woman. The night is young and yet I've already given you the orgasms you requested."

Taina pushed her head under his arm and he kissed her and held her close. The room was dark—Taina had made sure of that—lit only by the faint starlight which now entered the uncurtained window. "I'm pretty sure I'm not going to let you leave this bed until we've moved into double digits." She nipped his chest playfully.

His grip on her tightened. "And I'm pretty sure I'm not going to let you leave my side ever again."

His words may have intended to be playful but they hung on the silence with a weight of meaning. They should have been comforting, should have been welcome but all she could think of was that would he want her if he knew what had happened?

She swallowed. "And I… I'll only leave if you want me to go. Otherwise I'm back to stay." She lifted her head to catch his gaze, so he could see how much she meant it. "Whether we have a child or not."

"I'm sorry. I handled everything so badly. But all along, you have to know, that there was only one thing that was every really important to me. I might have wanted the diamond company—of course I wanted to make a name for myself, to be someone, other than a prince of a country I'd never reign. But over and above all these things, I wanted you. Only *you*. Only *ever* you. I'll never ask you to go. Never."

She swallowed, suddenly nervous. "Never's a long time. And I'm not that same woman who left you. I was away over a year... things happened—"

He frowned. "What things? Tell me, Taina. I know you're keeping something from me."

"Nothing. I don't mean anything much. Just normal things." She tried to laugh it off, tried to move away but he held her tight.

"Tell me. Don't be afraid. I'll look after you. I'll sort it out, whatever it is."

"Maybe that's what I'm afraid of, Daidan."

She felt the power leave his arms before they dropped to his side. He looked away and she wished she'd never said anything, wished that the moment had continued.

He swung his legs to the floor and sat on the bed for a moment, with his head in his hands, before rising and dressing.

She sat up. "Where are you going?"

He didn't turn to face her. "Work. There's always work to do. You sleep."

She reached for his hand and he squeezed it without turning around. "Daidan." She had to make him stop. She had to see what was in his eyes. She couldn't bear it that she'd broken that moment, when he'd opened his soul to her and she'd thrown it back in his face. "Daidan, please, look at me." Irrationally she felt as if he were to look her in the face, she could eradicate those last words of hers by sheer force of will alone.

But then he looked at her and the sadness and frustration she saw there robbed her of speech.

He turned his palms upwards in a helpless gesture, as if to say "you see?", shook his head and left the room.

And in that moment she knew she had to tell him every-thing—that not telling him all the facts was worse. He could be imagining things that had never happened. Imagining she'd never loved him, and never *would* love him. It was best that he knew the truth. She wouldn't name names. Just tell him what had happened to her. What it was that had made her return, wanting a baby so desperately.

She pressed her hand against her stomach. She might be pregnant already for all she knew. They'd only made love twice before tonight but she'd been at her most fertile and each time he'd come so fiercely into her, as if to claim her for his own again, that she'd felt he'd made her his in more ways than one.

She walked into the bathroom and turned on the shower. She caught sight of herself in the mirror under the glare of the bathroom light. Under that light she could see what she'd hoped to keep from Daidan, but what she now knew she had to tell him. Her fingers traced the telltale silvery stretch marks down her stomach. Then she looked up suddenly into eyes that were afraid. What would he do when she told him she'd already had a child?

CHAPTER 6

$\mathcal{M}$a'in was basking under brilliant sunshine when Taina and Daidan landed. Taina was treated like royalty in Finland, by virtue of being the only daughter of one of the country's wealthiest families but she'd never been treated like actual royalty. Her previous experience paled into insignificance.

Paparazzi lined the arrivals hall and Taina was glad she hadn't dressed down for the occasion. Daidan appeared to be totally comfortable with the fuss and attention around their arrival and for the first time Taina saw him in a different light. He'd dressed in robes for arriving in Ma'in. More comfortable, he'd said. And also because Tariq, the king and his older brother, was a traditionalist. Besides, the people liked it. It was fitting. Whatever the reasons, Taina thought Daidan looked sensational in the long white robes. They made his tall, lean body look taller somehow, and his dark complexion more exotic. He truly looked like a prince.

They were soon driving in a stretch limo down the wide avenue lined with exclusive boutiques at the end of which the royal palace sat, white and gleaming in the mid-day sun,

The avenue of date palms that lined the pink-tinted procession-way provided welcome shade. Under their graceful branches, rainbows flickered as water sprang up from hidden irrigation pipes to keep the beds of white flowers fresh.

As they got out the car two tall men, both dressed in flowing white robes, came down to greet them. One, smiling and amiable, was slightly ahead of the other more austere and dignified one.

"Daidan," the younger, sunnier Sahmir said, gripping Daidan by the shoulders and pulling him to him in a big brotherly hug. "Good to see you. How have you been?" And then he spotted Taina who'd just got out the car and stood behind Daidan, suddenly feeling very shy.

"Taina! What an unexpected surprise." He glanced at Daidan. "You didn't tell us to expect Taina!"

Daidan shrugged. "You'd find out soon enough. Anyway, it was a last minute decision."

Tariq meanwhile had gone straight toward Taina and taken her hand and kissed it. "Taina, it is a real pleasure and honor to have you with us. Thank you for coming. We, as Daidan's family, truly appreciate it."

Taina was touched by the big man's warmth and gentleness. He moved aside so Sahmir could greet her with a kiss on both cheeks. For a moment she marveled at the difference between the three men.

Then she looked up at Daidan and she saw such a heated gaze that she momentarily forgot the other two men and accepted his outstretched hand. Once he had her by his side he turned to his brothers. "Taina has returned to Helsinki," he said simply. Trust Daidan to say "Helsinki" instead of "me". But it looked as if the brothers understood fully.

"Good," said Tariq.

"Didn't think this was a social visit before she returned to wherever it was. Where were you again, Taina?"

She smiled and shrugged. It all seemed a long way behind her now. "Nowhere important." By the look on Daidan's face he liked the answer.

Taina had been to many beautiful and extraordinary places all over the world but, as they walked into the palace, she thought she'd never seen anything like this before. Their footsteps echoed on the marble floor as they entered a large reception area, decorated in cream and gold. The walls soared up two stories high, with each story framed by a series of gold-trimmed balconies. The building and its furnishings were on a scale of glamor and riches she'd never before experienced.

And then there were the people—many fully robed—who bowed respectfully as the King and his family passed by.

"Taina!" She turned to face Tariq. "My wife, Cara, will be sorry not to have been here to greet you but we didn't know you were coming and she's busy with the baby. However I know she'll want to meet you as soon as possible. As will my three children from my first marriage."

"That's Tariq's way of saying, 'prepare to be bombarded with questions by his kids,'" said Sahmir. "Rory's and my first baby is due next month. We got married a couple of months ago. You won't be able to stop her from meeting you as soon as she hears the news, either."

"Oh, congratulations. Daidan didn't tell me you were expecting."

Sahmir glanced at Daidan. "Daidan keeps a lot to himself," he said wryly.

Daidan shrugged. "Personal matters should be kept personal."

Sahmir clapped Daidan on the back. "Didn't anyone tell you that family is personal?"

"If you care to freshen up and go to your room, Taina," said Tariq. "Cara will call you shortly."

"That would be lovely." And she was sure it would be, even though she felt something of an impostor. These two women were happily married to Daidan's brothers and she— she was married, but only just. What would they make of her?

"Daidan"—Tariq turned to his brother—"take your beautiful wife to your suite and we'll catch up shortly. Welcome back. It's been too long."

Daidan led her out through a beautiful courtyard full of fountains and luxuriant flowers, bushes and trees. The smell of pungent flowers and damp soil was a relief after the dry heat outside.

"You didn't tell me it was all so beautiful," she said as they walked down a corridor with open arched windows to one side, in which fragrant climbers drifted in the desert breeze. "It's like a paradise. I can't believe you prefer to live in Finland when you have all this."

He stopped by a dark wooden door, studded with large nails. "I don't have all this. That is the point. This is all Tariq's. He was groomed to be king by my grandfather and father." He looked around at the grandeur. "None of this is mine." Then he looked at her. "And I wouldn't want it anyway. Finland is my home like this never was."

She frowned. "But Sahmir isn't the king and he seems quite happy."

"My younger brother is not me."

She couldn't help grinning. "In that he's charming, smiling and friendly?"

"Exactly." He returned her grin. "But he's also created a new life for himself in his wife's country in southern Europe. He spends half his time there, and half in Ma'in." He opened the door for her and she stepped inside their suite.

"Oh my!" She dropped her handbag onto the sofa and

walked over to the open windows. "Daidan, this is like a dream."

He followed her to the window which looked out over the internal courtyard. Above the tops of the palms and the wing of the palace opposite, the sea was visible—a brilliant strip of azure. He didn't answer but simply stood behind her. Then she felt his touch on her arm. "Thank you for coming. It means a lot."

She turned to face him. "It's my pleasure. Thank you for inviting me."

He smiled. "We're both being terribly polite for a married couple."

"Ah, that's because we've not been together long. Hardly at all as a married couple."

"So we're still in our courtship phase then."

"Definitely."

"And how do you know this?"

Should she tell him? "Because my heart trips a beat when you enter the room; because everyone else pales into insignificance beside you; and then, when you look at me, I feel a fluttering in my stomach of pure desire."

He'd pulled her to him, lifting her chin with his finger, and brought his lips to hers in a gentle and tender kiss. "Hold that thought until later," he murmured against her lips. "Because, now noisy children and curious sisters-in-law await."

"Do you ride?" asked Aurora, Sahmir's wife, trying to ease her heavily pregnant body into a more comfortable position as she accepted a non-alcoholic pre-dinner drink. The afternoon had passed pleasantly with them all getting to know each other and evening had now fallen and dinner was about to be served.

"No," Taina replied. "No, I never learned. I was brought up in Helsinki and when we went to our country home"—she shrugged—"we swam in summer and skied in winter. My father didn't keep horses. How about you?"

Cara laughed. "Rory's never off her horse when she's here."

"Nor at home." Rory twisted her thick coil of hair and pulled it to one side. "For half the year we live in the principality of Roche. Which borders France," she added by way of explanation.

"Oh, I'm often in Paris."

"Ever come to the south?"

"Rarely."

"Then you must start. It's very beautiful. And much warmer than Helsinki, I bet."

Taina grinned, liking the French woman's directness. "I'm sure you're right. It depends on work but I'll talk with Daidan and—" At that moment Daidan walked over and put his arm possessively around her waist.

"Did I hear my name mentioned?" he asked.

Rory grinned. "Of course. That's all we talk about when we're on our own—our husbands—or so you'd all like to believe."

"Then I'll leave again so you can enjoy talking about us." He ignored Rory's indignant grunt, kissed Taina on the cheek and rejoined Tariq who was watching Sahmir play with Tariq's children.

Cara smiled and lightly placed her hand on Taina's arm. "I'm so happy you came—Daidan's a different man when you're around."

"That's love," said Rory with a knowing grin.

Taina's smile faltered but she was saved from embarrassment by Cara who turned to Rory. "Let's go into the dining room. I'm sure the kids are hungry by now. Taina, would you tell the men?"

Taina walked up the long reception room, with its thick plush carpets and lush furnishings to where Tariq and Daidan stood. "Dinner is served."

Daidan and Taina followed Sahmir, Tariq and Tariq's children into the dining room and for the first time in her life Taina felt she belonged to a proper family. It might be a royal family but, with all its sibling teasings, warmth and chaos, it was still a real family. And it was hers.

TAINA DIDN'T THINK she'd ever seen Daidan so relaxed, despite his earlier protestations that Finland was more home to him than Ma'in. With his dark coloring and white robes, he looked both alien and familiar at the same time. While each of the brothers was different they were, without doubt, brothers. It was so strange seeing Daidan in a family setting. In Finland he'd always been the outsider. That was partly what had attracted her to him. Someone so different to everyone else she knew. He was right. That difference had been part of the initial attraction. But only initial. Now she saw him as a family man and her as part of that same family. It felt good.

Sahmir bent toward her. "A penny for your thoughts."

She frowned.

"A quaint English expression I picked up when I visited my cousins there," continued Sahmir.

"Ah. Well, my thoughts probably aren't even worth a penny."

"You are too humble." He glanced over at Daidan, noting her focus. "I'm betting they're centered on my handsome older brother."

"Um." She grinned at Sahmir. "Maybe."

"It was strange seeing him without a woman by his side this past year. Before he left for Finland he always had a stream of women."

She felt a stab of jealousy. "I'm sure he wasn't short of dates."

"I'm sure he had no interest." He studied her for a few moments. "I hope I'm not speaking out of turn, but I'm really not sure if my brother is well versed in the emotion of love. I've a suspicion that if he feels something, he assumes you should know—that it doesn't require stating."

"Or maybe he simply doesn't have anything to communicate?"

"Oh, he has something to communicate all right. And maybe I, as a long-time lover of women, should be the one to say it?"

"Say what?"

"That he loves you heart and soul, that you're the only one for him. He knows it. I know. But I wonder if you know it?"

She looked at the fine white gold-edged porcelain in front of her and pursed her lips and nodded. "Deep down, I think I always have. But I didn't trust myself." She sighed and shook her head, looking at Sahmir ruefully. "You must think me such a fool."

He touched her hand with his. "I think you're anything but a fool." He glanced at Daidan. "Well, maybe a little for getting involved with my complex brother." He gave a short laugh. "But you're good for each other. I can see that. And I certainly don't think you're a fool. I'm sure you had your reasons to do what you did. And you certainly don't have to tell me them."

"It would take too long." They watched as Daidan listened to Tariq's eldest daughter, Saarah, talk. By the looks of her animated face she was regaling him with the same tales she'd overheard her telling Rory about the antics of her favorite rock band. Things which ordinarily Daidan would have no time for, and less still have any interest in. But he was smiling kindly at his niece, letting her talk and nodding every now and then, allowing her to share her interests and enjoying her company. "Seeing Daidan here, among his family, is a bit of a revelation."

Sahmir followed her gaze across the room. "Really, why?"

"He seems so… patient and attentive."

"He loves his nieces—Saarah and little Eshal—and his one lone nephew, Gadiel. Although I hope Rory and I might provide another nephew for him to dote on soon."

"Or niece," Taina added.

"Indeed. Either are welcome. But Daidan's always loved children. I'm surprised it's taken him so long to have any."

He glanced at Taina then, suddenly realizing what he'd just said. Taina tried to smile reassuringly but thought she'd probably failed judging by Sahmir's look of discomfort.

"He's just so black and white at home, in Finland."

"He was always like that here. It's only"—continued Sahmir—"really since the birth of Eshal that Daidan's become less black and white about everything, less rigidly controlled. She'd charm anyone."

She frowned. "The control masks a volatile temper. He hit someone once—it could have ended very badly."

"Oh yes. Daidan's always had a temper but he's learned to control it as he's got older. He certainly looks more chilled and happy than I've seen him in a long time."

"What happened to make him so unhappy at home? To make him want to forge a life outside of Ma'in?"

"It was because of our parents—each had their favorite child. Unfortunately the rigid Daidan wasn't pliant enough for our mother—unlike me. And he wasn't the first born which made my grandparents raise Tariq with love and attention."

"But how about the King, your father? Didn't he have any room in his heart for Daidan?"

Sahmir frowned for a moment as he thought back. He shook his head. "No, I think my father only had time for Ensiyeh—our sister who died." He bit his lip and turned and looked across at Rory who was soothing a small baby. "If we have a girl, we'll name her after my sister."

"It's a beautiful name."

He smiled and turned back to Taina. "No, Daidan was basically left to his own devices. When Daidan should have been out having fun and getting up to mischief, he was studying diligently to make a name for himself. Our father gave him a hard time. He also gave Tariq a hard time, but Tariq had our grandparents to protect him and lived most of the time out in the desert at Qusayr Zarqa—our desert castle —with them. But Daidan? He had to take care of himself and it toughened him up too quickly. It made him unforgiving."

Taina nodded. She could see how Daidan had become the man she'd married. But his difficulty in forgiving didn't bode well for her. Because if he ever discovered her secrets, she doubted he'd forgive anyone concerned.

Just at that moment Rory came over and sat down beside Sahmir, stretching out her back and pushing her very pregnant stomach forward. Sahmir rubbed it for her. "Is he kicking?"

Rory sighed. "God knows what *she's* doing. Tap dancing I think." She caught Taina's eye. "Sahmir is convinced I'm carrying a boy and I just know it's a girl."

Taina felt a lump come to her throat as she tried to avoid looking at Rory's pregnant stomach and she nodded, not confident her voice wouldn't reveal the ache she was trying to hide.

"Ah, I'm kidding. I'm happy either way."

"Of course you are," said Rory as she kissed him. "Because you're just a big softy. Even if you prefer others to think of you as some kind of alpha male."

He gripped her hand and pulled her to him sharply and kissed her long and hard on the lips before releasing Rory flushed and breathless. "I'm alpha male where it counts, my darling, in our bedroom."

Taina looked away—uncomfortable by their hot desire for each other—and caught Daidan's eye who beckoned her over. She turned to Rory and Sahmir and excused herself, although she doubted they heard.

"Come, Taina, you'll be interested to hear what's happening to the lead singer of Saarah's favorite pop group."

Saarah didn't need further encouragement.

DAIDAN DRANK his wine and continued to watch Taina. It was as if two years had rolled back, and he was watching the woman he'd fallen in love with. Gone was the distance between her and other people, gone were the defenses. Her smile was ready and physically she had no choice but to accept the advances of Tariq's children, especially the youngest one, Eshal, who was exceptionally demonstrative in her affections.

Daidan laughed as Taina tried in vain to avoid eating a small chocolate that Eshal thought would be a great gift. Taina glanced at Daidan and grinned with a mouthful of chocolate. That grin curled into his stomach and nestled there.

At that moment Cara came over with the nurse. "Time you children went to bed," she said to the younger children. "And Eshal"—she grinned at Taina—"you must stop force-feeding people you love." Cara turned to Taina. "She seems to think the way to someone's heart is through their stomach. She's probably right though."

Slowly the children drifted off leaving Taina and Daidan alone.

Daidan watched Taina's expression as they left and was puzzled. She looked almost wistful. She held secrets. He knew she did. Not least about what happened to her necklace. Had she given it away? If so to whom? Why? Why had she given away the piece of jewelry that was so special to her family? Not to say valuable. He guessed he'd have to accept not knowing… at least in the short term. He finished his drink and rose. She looked up at him and in that moment he knew there was nothing more important than her… now.

He held out his hand and she rose and took it. He turned to Tariq and Cara—Sahmir and Rory had retired to bed—who were entertaining the few friends who remained. "Good night, Cara, Tariq. And thank you."

They both rose. "Our pleasure," said Cara, kissing Taina warmly on the cheeks before doing the same to him. Although Cara was shorter than Taina, there was a subtle radiance about her that made her just as beautiful as the other women, Daidan thought.

"And will you be able to stay the week? We can show you the progress we've made on the regeneration in the desert," said Tariq.

"Only a few more days and then we must return to Finland. The launch isn't far away and we've still a lot of work to do."

"Thank you so much for coming, Taina." Cara glanced at Daidan. "I've never seen him look so happy."

Daidan looked over to see Taina looking at him as if she'd made up her mind about something.

"Are you suggesting, Cara, that the presence of my wife has improved my mood?"

Cara lifted her chin and grinned. "Most definitely." She stood on tiptoe and kissed his cheek. "You only look forbidding now, rather than positively scary."

"So long as I never look approachable. A man has to have some standards." He turned to Tariq. "Now you must excuse my wife and me—we've had a busy week."

"Of course. Sleep well and we'll see you in the morning."

Once outside, Daidan stopped and pulled her into his arms. "I've wanted to do this all night."

"What?" she whispered, lifting her face to his.

"This..." He bent down and pressed his lips to hers, closing his eyes as he became drenched in her perfume, the essence of her. He wanted to prolong the kiss but now was not the time.

"Um," she moaned.

"Come on, let's get back to our suite."

It was a winding walk back to their rooms through perfumed gardens and colonnaded walkways. Daidan looked at it through Taina's eyes and appreciated its beauty in a way that he'd never done growing up in the palace.

She tugged on his hand and halted at a particularly beautiful fountain—small, set in a jewel-like formation of decorated tiles. The greenery hung all around them, but the water and the fountain and tiles formed the central focal point and were devoid of plants. The water ran bright and sparkling in the starlight, the sound of it running over the black and gold tiles providing a contrast to the heat of the night.

"I've never seen anything so beautiful." Taina went and sat on the edge of the circular fountain. Then she laughed. "It's in the shape of a lily of the valley, just like the kielo—like Mama's piece..." She didn't look up, suddenly realizing her mistake of reminding him of the invaluable piece she'd given away.

He walked up to her and caressed her shoulder. "It's okay.

What's done, is done. If we've a hope of a future together we need to be able to speak freely." He pulled her to standing and took both her hands in his. "Taina, I need there not to be secrets between us. We need a future where we trust each other. Okay?"

She nodded but was silent. And when she looked up, he saw sadness in her eyes. He exhaled roughly. He didn't want to see sadness in her eyes.

He must have conveyed his feelings to Taina. "And that's what I want, too. But let's not rush anything. I've only just returned. Please, Daidan, give me time."

And how could he do anything else other than agree with her? At that moment when she looked up with her pleading eyes and her pale face as inviting as the moon flower, and as perfect. "Taina, I'd give you anything."

"I just want a little time. That's all. Nothing else."

He narrowed his eyes. "Nothing?"

Her lips curled up into a deliciously sexy smile and she raised an eyebrow. "Well, now you ask, maybe I should be more demanding."

She hooked her hand around his neck and brushed her lips against his skin. He closed his eyes as he let the sensations fill his blood. That was all she did and it was all she needed to do.

He grabbed her hand and they ran down the remaining corridors to their suite. He swung open the heavy teak doors and, without waiting to turn on the lights, walked across the marble floor to the canopy bed from which pure white silk linings were draped. They shifted slightly in the welcome fragrant breeze that came in through the open windows.

There, he thrust his fingers into her hair and held her head still so he could drink her in. In the darkness he couldn't see the details, only her form, herself.

"I can't believe you're back in my arms, Taina. I still can't believe it."

"Nor me. I'm so sorry, Daidan."

"It wasn't your fault. It was all mine. I gave no thought to the fact you'd see an arranged marriage differently than I did. And I should have known." He brushed his lips against hers and her mouth opened, wanting more. "You should never be forced to do anything you don't want to do. And I'll make sure it never happens again. I promise. Nothing must come between us again."

He wondered as to her slight frown but his kiss soon swept it away.

He carefully undid her long dress and drew it away from her body and turned her around.

"I want to see you."

She hesitated.

He kissed her. "I don't want anything between us any more, not lies, not clothes, nothing."

"Tomorrow. You'll see me tomorrow when morning comes. But for tonight, feel me, taste me, just as you used to do."

And he did.

TAINA WOKE UP WITH A START. Bright sunlight poured in unimpeded through the open windows. She turned to look at Daidan who was still asleep. Her heart thumped and she stared at the distance between her gown and the bed. She'd have to walk across the bright sunlight in which everything was plainly visible.

Last night her decision had seemed so logical, so easy. Her faith in Daidan's acceptance hadn't wavered. But it did, now, in the cold light of day.

Maybe she could delay it. Maybe if she didn't make a sound Daidan would remain asleep.

Carefully she pulled back the cover. She wondered for a moment if she could wrap it around herself, but that would mean pulling it from Daidan and then he'd be bound to wake up and wonder why she was walking across the large room wrapped in a sheet. It wouldn't end well. No, her only hope was to quietly slip out of bed naked.

She eased herself toward the edge of the mattress and then stopped when Daidan turned over and flung one arm over her stomach. She froze and watched his face. He was still asleep. Seemed he wanted to check she was still there even in his sleep. And no wonder. It would be a long time until they felt totally sure of each other.

She covered herself again, just in case she awoke him, and carefully lifted his hand and put it back on the mattress. He didn't stir. This time she moved more quickly, slipping out of the bed and padding softly across the room.

"Where are you going?" Daidan's voice rumbled sexily from behind her. She kept on walking.

"Just to the bathroom."

"Well, come back to me afterwards."

She felt her body respond to the invitation but she continued to walk, scooping up her dress as she went. "If you're lucky," she responded. She just made it to the bathroom before he got to her.

She closed the door behind her and leaned back against it, catching sight of herself in the mirror. How the hell was she going to get out of this? She looked around. Damn, there was no robe. She looked at her dress. She could hardly put this on again.

A few minutes later she exited the bathroom, clutching her dress in front of her.

"Baby, come here."

She stood uncertainly, clutching her dress in front of her stomach. "Don't we have an engagement in an hour?"

"I'll re-arrange it. I have other, more important things on my mind."

"Daidan… I…"

"Taina." He stretched out and grabbed her hand. "Come here." She fell onto the bed, her dress crushed between him and her stomach. He tried to move it away but she held on to it. She could see the precise moment when he knew something was wrong. He frowned and looked at her with intent focus. "What's wrong? What are you doing?"

She shook her head.

"Tell me." He kissed her when she continued not to speak. "You can tell me anything."

Maybe she could? Maybe he really had changed in the time she'd been away.

He pulled her into his arms and drew the covers over her and kissed her tenderly and smoothed her cheek with his thumb. "Taina, tell me."

She swallowed and drew in a deep calming breath. "When I first returned you asked me a question which I didn't answer."

He frowned. "I think I asked you many which you didn't answer. Which one are you referring to?"

"You asked me why I wanted a baby so much, why I'd risk humiliating myself by asking you for one."

He nodded. "And?"

She pushed back the cover and knelt on the bed facing him, letting last night's dress fall to one side. But he didn't look down as she'd imagined. His eyes were still focused intently on hers. He took both her hands in his and stroked the backs of them, encouraging her to continue.

"The answer is that something happened. Something that made me realize how much I would like to have a child."

Still he said nothing so she continued.

"When you lose something, something you never even thought you wanted, then sometimes…"—she sucked in a deep breath—"sometimes it makes you realize just how much you want it."

"What did you lose?"

"A baby." The words emerged in a rushed whisper through her dry lips.

The grip of his hands hurt as he suddenly tightened them. "A baby?" His voice was as hoarse as hers. He pulled away and jumped up, pulling on his robe. Then he stood, hands on hips, looking out the window, unseeing. He shook his head.

She rose, naked now, and walked behind him, and hesitantly touched his shoulder. He'd said he'd understand. He'd told her to trust him. And she had. There was no going back now.

He spun around and she stepped away instinctively under the heat of his glare. "A baby? You had a relationship after you left me at our wedding? You had a baby from that relationship?"

She nodded mutely.

"Where's the child now? Don't tell me you've left it somewhere being looked after by someone else?"

She wanted to turn away, run from the glare of his gaze, from the glare of the exposing daylight. Only then did he look down and see what she'd been trying to hide. He shook his head and his eyes traced the tell-tale lines of her stretch marks. "So they're what you've been trying to hide from me. You know, I thought you'd become shy, that you were nervous. But you were simply trying to conceal the truth." She flinched under the look of disdain in his eyes.

He backed away from her and she was left looking out into the blinding morning light, the sun reflecting harshly off the white buildings below them and the sky which was almost white.

"You were unfaithful to me, to our wedding vows, to our agreement. How could you have done that, Taina?"

There was a limit to the truth and Taina had reached it.

She turned and folded her arms in front of her feeling vulnerable. There was so much to be said and so little she could say, not without hurting him further. She shrugged and shook her head helplessly.

"And this man, who is he?"

She shook her head. "He's nothing."

"Right," he said with a steely tone. "You had a baby with a man who means nothing to you."

She nodded. After all, it was the truth.

"Is it over?"

"What?" She couldn't think of what he was speaking.

"Your relationship with the child's father."

She flinched at the idea that she'd had any kind of emotional relationship with the child's father. "Yes. Absolutely." A sob rose from deep inside her throat, constricting it as she watched his lip curl into contempt.

"I'd never have believed it of you. I don't know you at all, do I?"

She shook her head, trying to deny what he so reasonably believed.

"Where's the baby?" he asked her again.

She kept her eyes focused on the bright light outside. A sharp gleam of sunlight flashed as the rising sun hit an open window, making her eyes water. "She's dead."

"Dead? Ah," he scoffed. "So the baby died and you now feel bereft so you thought you'd return to your husband and demand a replacement. Well, I hope last night did it for you, because it won't be happening again." He stopped before the bathroom. "Get showered, get dressed. We'll be leaving as soon as my nephew's celebrations are over."

He cast one quick glance over her, standing naked before the white light of the morning, shook his head and walked to the door. There he stopped but he didn't turn to face her. "Are you going to tell me who the father is?"

She shook her head. "I can't."

"You're protecting him."

She shook her head and he went out and closed the door behind him without another word.

No, she thought to herself, *I'm protecting you.*

CHAPTER 7

*T*aina looked out the window with eyes that stung from lack of sleep. They were passing across the coastline of Estonia. Soon they'd see the waterways, lakes, and forests of Finland through the misty morning light. She closed her eyes. Thank God they were back. The flight had been a nightmare. Daidan had barely spoken two words to her. The bedroom lay unused. Daidan had remained in his office working—barking commands at people if they entered his office and glaring at anyone else—while she'd remained seated, trying to figure out how the hell she could make things better between them when she couldn't tell him the one thing he wanted to know. Who the baby's father had been. How she'd been conceived.

If she told him Daidan's world would come crashing around his shoulders. He'd react with violence no matter how much he thought he was in control. If he'd sent a man to hospital for flirting with her, how much worse would this be? And it would impact the business as well. She couldn't do that to him on top of everything else. She just had to hope that he'd somehow come to terms with not knowing and carry on. Because already she missed the man she'd come to know—missed his companionship, missed his warmth, and his loving. He'd come round, she told herself. He'd come round. But she felt cold inside. Cold and afraid that he never *would* come round.

"JUST FIND HIM." Daidan slammed down the phone and stood up from his desk, pushing his fingers through his short hair. Another trail had hit a dead end. He twisted round his computer and entered a few commands. He'd gotten further than he had done in the past. Because he knew she'd had a baby and so that narrowed down the search. But still he couldn't nail down what had happened. Who'd she'd been with. There had been no scandal, no relationships that had hit the papers, no lover that anyone knew anything about. She'd been the same dignified person, attending parties, leaving alone. Not once had she slipped up that he could see. He was crazy with jealousy. All the time he hadn't known that she'd had other men, he'd been able to persuade himself that, like him, she hadn't had an affair during their separation. But now he didn't have that luxury. She'd confirmed the truth. And he knew it was the truth. He could see it in her eyes and besides, it made sense. She'd lost the child, she wanted another.

From what he'd read losing a child, even if it was an unwanted one, could be a painful psychological experience. But it turned out it wasn't painful for only her. It was beyond pain for him, too.

He sat back down at the computer, searching through the photographs that his contacts had found for him. Not once had she been photographed with another man other than in a group function. Only by herself, or with other women. He had his staff going over the receipts once more in the offices but they found nothing new. Only receipts from Aspen, the Maldives and New York. And there the trail stopped suddenly.

It seemed the only aberrant behavior from Taina was leaving him on their wedding day. Apart from that her public life was as immaculate as she wanted it to appear. But only he and she knew different. He'd always thought of her as "his" Taina, "his" woman, even when she was away from him, but now, as irrational as he knew it to be, he felt she wasn't "his" any more. And the thought killed him. If he could only lay his hands on the man who did this to her he'd— He stopped abruptly at that thought, suddenly realizing that that was exactly why Taina would never tell him. She was afraid of what he'd do. Afraid he'd lose his control and end up in jail. He couldn't blame her. It nearly happened once before. But once was enough. He'd changed, even if she didn't realize it.

Trying to re-focus, he went through his emails. Yet another report of something a Russian had said to one of his staff. This time in New York. The repeated threats were becoming less veiled, more explicit. The threats, together with what Sahmir had said, had meant he'd have to step up security, especially leading up to the launch. Nothing must go wrong. He'd waited his whole life for the chance to create something of his own and he was determined not to have it ruined now. The business might have started off as Taina's family's business—and that image was still being used as its brand—but he now owned half, and the infrastructure and plans for expansion were all down to him. If he hadn't stepped in when he had, the company would still be content to be a big fish in the small pond of Finland. Under his control, it was about to go global.

He took one more frustrated look at the computer and paced over to the door. The landing lights were lit, so he walked out of the office toward Taina. She sat with her dark glasses on but she looked up as he approached. He didn't say anything, simply took the seat opposite her and clicked on the belt. He rubbed his stubbly chin and gazed stubbornly out the window.

She leaned over toward him. "Is this how it's going to be, Daidan? You ignoring me? Christ, just look at me."

He looked then. All he could see was her pale face and her sunglasses. "What's the point, eh, Taina?"

Mistaking his words, she pushed up her sunglasses onto the top of her head.

He shook his head. "That's not going to help. Even without your sunglasses I don't see you. I thought I did. But I don't. You've a shield between you and the rest of the world. You might have set it up as a protection growing up but it's become a part of you now. Something to hide your true self behind so that no one can know you." He sat back with a sigh and looked out the window again. "And that includes me."

"I've obviously spent too much time with you then, haven't I? Because you've turned self-protection into an art form." Taina let the glasses drop onto her nose and turned away.

TAINA SANK BACK into the leather-lined seats of Daidan's Porsche convertible and looked moodily out the window.

"I don't know why you decided to get rid of Papa's old Daimler."

Daidan flexed his hands around the steering wheel and gripped it more tightly as he negotiated the rush-hour traffic of central Helsinki. "Precisely because of those three things: it was your father's, it was old, and it was a Daimler."

"Nothing wrong with a Daimler," she muttered, unable to argue on the first two points.

She'd begun the flight back from Ma'in distressed by Daidan's reaction, but with each passing hour she was beginning to get more and more annoyed. Yes, she could see why he'd be so angry—he'd always been jealous and possessive—but there was no way she was going to open up that part of her life to him. She simply couldn't. It had been destructive then and had the potential to be even more so now. She'd told him it was a brief relationship—it had nearly killed her simply using that word—and that it had been a mistake, a mistake with long-standing consequences. Everyone made mistakes, she thought miserably as she continued to look out the window. Didn't they?

She looked at him once more. She could tell by the flicker of his lids that he was aware of her gaze but he didn't glance at her or speak.

"We can't continue like this."

He grunted.

"Apart from anything else we have to work together."

He still didn't meet her gaze, just continued to stare straight ahead, even though the traffic was stationary. "Since when have you been so concerned about work?"

"Since I accepted your counter proposal."

He turned to her then, eyeing her coolly. "Ah yes, the proposal that would see you work for the company from which you derive your wealth, and replace your baby with a new one."

She glared at him. "My baby died from complications a few weeks after she was born. She made me realize I want to have more children but there's no way that she'll ever be replaced, she was her own person. I'd never imagined you could be so insensitive."

"Then we're both learning things about each other, aren't

we? I'm insensitive and you're unfaithful. What a great team we make."

"It didn't have to be like this, Daidan. Not if you and my father had treated me like a person, rather than a chattel."

"That's ridiculous. I never treated you like a chattel."

"What would you call negotiating the terms of our marriage as a business deal?"

"Sensible."

She turned aside and looked out the window. She frowned. "Hey, where are we going? This isn't the way to the apartment, or the business."

"We're going to be based on the island from now on."

"What? Why?"

"The risk is too great for us to continue to work in the city."

"For the plans, or for me?"

He glared at her. "Both. I've had everything moved over to the island. We can work from there."

"You see!" she said angrily. "That's precisely what I mean. You take these unilateral decisions, without even discussing them with me."

"There's nothing to discuss."

"Then there's no hope for us. If we can't even discuss the simplest of things, there's no future."

"I'm surprised it's taken you this long to work that out. Do you want to leave, want to go back to your boyfriend?"

"I don't have a boyfriend, as you well know. Daidan! Just listen to me. I can't tell you the details, I just can't, but I'm telling you the truth. There was nothing between me and the father of my child."

He grunted with disbelief.

Her eyes narrowed. "You know what I mean. Please, Daidan, stop this. We can't go on like it. Unless…"

"Unless?"

"Unless you wish to stop what we're doing? You want me to leave? I told you I'd leave if you asked. Now's your chance."

"Do you want to?"

She shook her head.

"Then we continue as we are."

"Only if you leave this behind you."

"Only if you promise me that there's no more surprises. There's nothing more that happened. I need to be able to trust you."

"There's nothing more you need to know."

His eyes narrowed suspiciously for a moment before he turned away. For a moment Taina wondered if her answer would satisfy him. Then he turned to her. "We're here." Whatever his thoughts he was obviously not going to express them.

THE BOAT BOUNCED on the small waves that peppered the gulf. And Taina's grip of the rail tightened as she watched the island approach with the ruins of the castle where her family had defended their lands in medieval times looming over it. Seemed times hadn't changed that much. The castle and island, which would be the location for the big launch, was still a place of retreat and, to her, a place of imprisonment. Now more than ever.

She glanced at Daidan who sat reading the paper on the deck. "I'll need to return to the city in a few days."

"No."

"But surely we'll be moving back and forth, right?"

"Wrong. I can't risk it. Not with so much going on. I want to keep a tight control over every aspect of this launch and we can do that better on site. Our key staff will come to the island during the day and the jewelry will be brought by armored guard on the day of the launch itself. It's only for another week. Once the launch is over everything will be back to normal."

"You really think someone is out to sabotage the launch? Or do you suspect it's more personal?"

He didn't speak for a few moments. "It's possible and I'm not willing to take the risk."

"Do you think it's something to do with the Russians? I realize they must be annoyed that our new safety measures show them in a bad light and they might lose business, but my father and the head of the Russian company always respected each other, even if they were competitors. Surely they wouldn't turn their back on our joint history?"

Again Daidan remained silent and she racked her brains to figure out what he was getting so paranoid about. For a brief moment she wondered if he was keeping anything from her but then she dismissed the idea. No, he was just being the same controlling man as her father had been.

"People don't always behave rationally. I'd thought you'd have realized that, Taina. We're working from the island until the launch. There's nothing you can do but accept it. It is as it is."

The boat docked at the jetty and Daidan spoke to the captain while Taina disembarked and walked up to the house, almost hidden by the overhanging trees. With each echoing footstep she took along the wooden jetty, the feeling of dread grew. She recognized it because she'd experienced that same sense of apprehension growing up on the island. But this time it appeared the threat was real—whether to her or the company, she didn't know—and this time she had no idea from which direction the attack was coming.

BY MIDWEEK she felt as if she were going crazy. A few staff came and were gone by six in the evening. They, and the household staff, were the only people she saw. The boat was the only way out and Daidan's had the key to that. She was effectively trapped in her own home—just as she had been growing up.

Yes, she loved working on the jewelry collection, combining her initials with her mother's in a new center-piece to the range. The heartache remained but she was managing it. And she enjoyed working with Daidan's team on the launch arrangements and whatever marketing was required. What she couldn't manage was the feeling of being trapped against her will.

She decided to finish early and went for a walk around the small island, through the woodland and around to the old castle to see how the work was coming on. A new theatre stage had been built to replace the old one which had been used by her parents and her grandparents before them. Up until the past few years their family had held occasional festivals at the castle, taking advantage of its amazing acoustics and stunning natural setting.

By the time she returned it was nearing six and as she walked across the lawn at the rear of the property she heard a strange wailing sound, followed by silence. It was only when she reached the house and the sound continued, this time unabated, that she realized what it was—the sound of a baby crying. It struck to the heart of her and she dropped the flowers she'd picked and went running up the path. She was met by one of the staff trying to soothe a baby who was crying lustily. Taina recognized the baby—she was the daughter of her PA, Livvy.

"Where's Livvy?" asked Taina as she walked up to the baby, whose cries were growing more insistent with each passing minute.

"In with Daidan. Her babysitter let her down and she had to drop some papers off."

"Give her to me." Instinctively Taina wanted to comfort the child and she held out her hands to the baby. The baby was handed to her but didn't stop crying. She rocked her and walked her up and down the hallway. Then she gave the baby the dummy that someone offered and the baby snuggled against her, instantly soothed.

Taina was lost in a flood of maternal feeling for the infant. She couldn't stop looking at her as she held her close, comforting her like she'd never been able to comfort her own child.

Suddenly she was aware that a hush had fallen on the room. She turned to see Daidan standing at the open study door, staring at her, an unguarded look of sadness in his eyes. Immediately Livvy came toward her. "I'm so sorry. I thought she'd be okay. She's just been fed, you see."

"No problem." Taina looked down at the baby in her arms. "No problem at all."

Then Daidan came up to her and put his arm gently around her shoulders. "Livvy wants to go now."

Taina looked up suddenly. She hadn't noticed Livvy had her arms outstretched waiting for Taina to return her baby to her. "Sure. Sorry, I…"

Livvy took the baby from her with crooning sounds which cut Taina to the quick. She turned away abruptly.

"Your baby's perfect, Livvy," said Daidan to fill the awkward silence. "I just hope our baby will be as beautiful."

Then all eyes looked up to Daidan who was only looking at Taina.

"You're expecting a baby?" asked Livvy.

"Not yet," he said without taking his eyes from Taina. "But we will be. Very soon."

Taina nodded and bit her lip to stop it from trembling.

Daidan might never forgive her for having a child with another man, but the way he was looking at her now, with that complex mixture of sadness, regret, and sympathy, made her realize he still had feelings for her and he'd give her what she yearned for so desperately.

She tucked her hair behind one ear and smiled as best she could at the young woman. "She wasn't any trouble. I'm glad you brought her. Daidan's right. She is beautiful. Bring her back any time." She turned to Daidan. "I have to go… I have some… work to do."

"Sure."

She managed to escape the room before the tears came. She went straight to her room and sat on the bed and put her head in her hands and sobbed. After her sobs subsided she was aware that a silence had fallen over the house. Then she heard approaching footsteps. Footsteps that stopped, right outside her room.

She closed her eyes, hoping Daidan would turn away—for it had to be him—hoping he wouldn't see her like this—broken and weak.

He knocked once. The door wasn't locked. He could have entered if he wished. She swung her legs off her bed and swiped the tears roughly from under her eyes and walked over to the door and opened it.

He searched her face and she tilted her chin, defying him to see her weakness.

"May I come in?" he asked.

She opened the door wide. "Of course."

He walked in and looked around. "It's a long time since I've been in your old room."

She closed the door and turned to him. "Really? And yet you've lived on the island since I've been away."

He glanced at her. "At weekends. When I wanted to get away. Maybe"—he nodded as if urging himself to tell the truth—"maybe when I wanted to feel close to you."

"My jeans… in my closet. You knew where they were."

"I missed you."

"And yet you let me go. And didn't follow me."

"You asked me to respect your wishes and I did." He paused. "And I've always regretted it. I should have followed you. I should have made you see that the arrangements I came to with your father didn't mean I didn't love you. I did. And I do."

Sadness swelled inside her, creating a lump in her throat. She pursed her lips and shook her head. "I wish you'd come after me when I left. I wish you'd told me. I believed the opposite was true."

"Yes, well"—he nodded briefly—"everything's easier with hindsight." He walked over to the window, leaned against the billowing curtains, and looked across to the city. "But I've learned from my mistakes." He looked at her. "I'm not going to let you get away again."

She knew what he meant, knew that he was simply saying he wasn't going to make the same mistake twice, so why did she feel uneasy? She laughed nervously. "Don't say it like that, Daidan. It makes me feel trapped."

"You know me. I'm no good at saying things smoothly. They always come out wrong. I just mean that I never want you to leave me again." He walked over to her and took her hands in his. "We've been given another chance. Let's take it and make the most of it—what's happened has happened and there's nothing either of us can do about it."

She exhaled roughly and looked down. "You can't believe how long I've waited to hear you say that."

He lifted her chin and kissed her so tenderly, so without ownership, as if the clock had been turned back to when they had no resentment, no past, no secrets between them. She melted into his arms and he held her tight, the kiss continuing, as the tension increased—their breathing coming harder, as his hands pushed up under her shirt, her skin goose-bumping under his touch, her hips shifting to him in reaction.

He pulled away too soon, his thumbs sweeping her cheeks. She gripped his hips and held them against hers, grazing his neck with her lips as she moved against his erection, telling him what she wanted in no uncertain terms. He didn't need any further encouragement and they fell to the bed, legs and arms and bodies entwined, as she fumbled with the buttons on his shirt. Before she'd reached the last one, he'd deftly undone her bra and pushed off her shirt and with a little wriggling her trousers landed on the floor.

As soon as he was naked she pulled away from underneath him. She was tired of being underneath, tired of being made love to. She straddled him and kissed him. "This time, I'm in charge," she whispered against his mouth. He fell back with a groan as she took charge, with both hands.

"You're always in charge," he said, his voice rough with desire. "You just don't know it."

She paused for a moment, thinking about his meaning, wondering whether he believed what he said, wondering if it were true.

"For God's sake, don't stop!"

She grinned as she continued her ministrations, his eyes closing only briefly before opening to meet her gaze, a gaze that did things to her, that made her take away her hands and lift her hips and drop down gently on top of him, watching him all the while. The intensity in those hooded eyes as they maintained a macho authority over her, even when she was on top, drove her harder. She leaned forward, gripped his shoulders with her hands, her breasts grazing his chest, her breath upon his face as she rode him until he was forced to close his eyes as he came. And when he came, he called out her name. Only then did she succumb to the waves of orgasm that she'd barely been able to keep at bay. She sat up, shifting her body for maximum satisfaction and crying out as a second wave slammed into her.

For a moment she thought she'd blacked out. Because suddenly she was in his arms, lying side by side, him still inside her, her legs clasping his waist. She closed her eyes as she half-listened to his murmured Arabic endearments of which she had no understanding. He continued to caress her, both inside and out, as her body responded to him, and the ripples of pleasure began once more.

Late into the night, they continued to make love while outside the birds sang and the late evening sunlight played over their bodies, slick with sweat, in the long midsummer twilight. It was only when the brief dusk that fell for an hour or so either side of midnight descended, that their love-making ceased and they drifted into sleep.

SHE LAY awake in the early morning and turned to see he'd gone. He was never there when she awoke. He needed little sleep and was always working. She knew these things and yet still she felt rejected every time she awoke to find him gone.

She turned over on the fine linen sheets to look out through the open window toward Helsinki. From here she could just make out the low-lying buildings surrounding the old city near the wharf, where her mother's studio/warehouse was. For years after her mother's death, she'd look out and think about her mother, and of how different things would have been if Taina had made a different choice at fourteen.

She thought of The Warehouse now. It had the working drawings she needed to finish off her project. She knew

Daidan would arrange for them to be brought to the island for her if she asked him. But what was she? A little girl who had to ask permission for everything?

She jumped out of bed and stretched. It was still early. Daidan would be at work in the library. The staff hadn't arrived at the island yet. She walked over to her wardrobe and pulled out sensible, warm clothes, rather than her elegant, expensive designer wear. She wouldn't need those where she was going this morning.

DAIDAN STILL HADN'T EMERGED from the library and Taina was able to pick up the key for the boat without him knowing. Not that he'd hidden it. She was sure that he wouldn't know that she was an excellent sailor. In their short time together, she'd never had to demonstrate it.

By the time she made her way down through the terraced gardens, dew was on the grass and birdsong filled the air. She had to get out of there. She walked quickly to the boatshed and unlocked it. She glanced up at the house briefly to see if the whirring of the electronic doors had stirred anyone. There was no sign of activity. Presumably Daidan was either on the phone, Skyping, or immersed in his work.

She knew the drill, the security, how to work the boat. She'd lived most of her life on the island and knew boating inside out. It had been her only escape. It had been on one of her expeditions that she'd first met Daidan. It seemed so long ago.

Quietly she maneuvered the boat out into the bay, making sure to keep close to the shoreline, under the trees whose branches dipped and dragged in the current. She winced at the sound of the motor in the quiet of the morning. As soon as she was around the headland she opened up the throttle and headed to Helsinki at full speed. She'd get those designs she wanted from her mother's studio in The Warehouse. And, more importantly, she'd get away from the island for a few hours.

DAIDAN PULLED the phone away from his ear, trying to figure out what the noise was he'd just heard above the conference call he was on. Then he heard it, a change in gear of a small boat—his boat. Taina! He jumped up and opened the dressing room door. It was empty. Damn!

"Taina!" he bellowed, but he knew it was no good. She'd taken the boat. He just knew it. "Taina!" he called again as the other end of the house. But her name echoed around the huge space, taunting him with its empty sound.

He dressed quickly and picked up his phone. He had a message. Just a brief text from her, just saying she needed to get away for a few hours. On her own. But where? He looked across the waters to Helsinki and saw several boats. He got the binoculars and focused on one in particular—the flag snapping jauntily in the breeze. It was the Mustonen pennant. He narrowed his gaze as he punched a number into his phone.

"Get a helicopter over to me straight away and then get yourself and a couple of the men over to the quay, *fast*. Taina's on her way over and she's no idea as to the trouble she could run into."

He slammed down the phone and looked over at the boat that grew smaller with each passing minute. She had no idea of the desperation of men whose livelihood their new company would impact on. No idea of the depths they'd stoop to. He just prayed that his men would get to her before the Russians.

CHAPTER 8

*T*aina couldn't remember the last time she'd made the crossing alone. But she hadn't forgotten what to do, how to operate the boat, how to glide it carefully into position at that part of the quay that had belonged to her family—a couple of miles from where Daidan preferred to keep his boats. The family quay was on the island of Katajanokka which was separated from the city of Helsinki by a narrow canal. It was here, amongst the grand old buildings, the awe-inspiring Uspenski Cathedral, and the leafy parks, that her mother's warehouse was situated. She needed to go there to pick up some design work. But that wasn't the only reason. She simply needed to go there—to make peace with her mother, and her past.

After docking, with the help of a couple of surprised waterside workers, she jumped up onto the quay. With no bag, just the keys to the boat and The Warehouse and her wallet slipped in her pockets, she walked toward her mother's warehouse. It was still early so the place was deserted. The summer holidays hadn't begun in earnest so visitors were few and far between.

She walked past beautiful nineteenth-century stone buildings, painted in the softest of chalky hues—lemon, blue, brown, ochre—all blending together, making this historic area also one of the most picturesque in Helsinki. The trees that lined the wide street were heavy with new leaf and barely moved in the still air. It was going to be a hot day— and a humid one. She continued walking a block until she arrived at the quarter where The Warehouse was. With the sea on one side, and a large park on the other, the historic red-brick warehouse and its neighbors stood in a prime position. The other warehouses had also been converted into restaurants, business centers and hotels. Normally there was a buzz about the place but now, with so few people around, Taina looked upon it with different eyes. She stopped under the shelter of the trees and looked up at its age-softened façade with its beautifully proportioned, arched windows. She lifted her gaze higher to the topmost window into which the early morning sun was shining. She pictured the sunny window seat on the other side where she used to sit and watch her mother draw by the light of the window on the northern slide of the building.

She couldn't remember the last time she'd seen the building from this angle. She always arrived by car, sweeping up the boulevard and being deposited directly outside. It seemed strange from this perspective. A shiver ran down her spine. She stepped forward to cross the street and then hesitated. She'd go to the hotel and grab a coffee before she went inside.

As soon as she entered the hotel she felt a slither of unease run down her spine. She stopped for a moment and looked around. Nothing seemed out of the ordinary. She used to come here often and the staff greeted her with their usual warmth. She shrugged. She must be imagining things.

She continued on her way to the rear of the hotel where

there was a small but exclusive café. After she placed her order she looked around, suddenly aware of the different accents and languages. In this quarter of Katajanokka, the pattern of industry had continued from the old days with a polyglot of import and export industries with nations from around the world. The Warehouse had been at the center of all this industry and so she was used to conversations being carried on around her in different languages and had become skilled in a few of them. But Russian, she'd never learned beyond the basics. And it was Russian she could hear now.

She turned and glanced at the group of men who were speaking in a low murmur. Even if she could understand Russian they were too far away for her to hear. The man in the group who was obviously in charge, sat back quietly as he listened to the other two men talk, but he wasn't looking at them. He was looking at her.

She turned away instantly. She was used to men looking at her, but not like that. There was no admiration in his eyes —they were too cold but still intent. He looked… dangerous. The word popped into her mind and sent a chill down her spine. She took the coffee and cake and, without turning back, walked quickly through the hotel and back into the sunshine.

She walked briskly to her building, and around the back, using the old key to unlock the black metal grille, before raising it and punching the security code into the keypad. The grille and key were effective but the warehouse also had state of the art security.

She closed the door firmly behind her and rolled her shoulders which she suddenly discovered were tense. She looked around the showroom. She felt inclined to stay there in the safety of the displays and computers, let the beautiful surroundings bathe over her like a warm balm. But that wasn't what she was here for.

Instead she walked to the rear of the showroom and up the old staircase that led to her mother's room. The morning sun slanted through the high arched windows and criss-crossed over the dark jewel-like colors of the rugs that were strewn over the waxed floor boards. Dust motes floated lazily in the warm air. Her mother had always been able to create a home from a building and her loyal staff had changed very little in the ten years she'd been gone.

She glanced toward the doors at the rear of the studio. They were firmly closed. She breathed a sigh of relief and walked around the room, picking up pieces, examining them and remembering why they had been special to her mother, before placing them carefully back where she'd found them. She could feel something of her mother there, but not in a menacing way anymore. She didn't know what had changed, but something had. Something in *her* had changed, she suddenly realized.

It was no longer solely her mother's studio, it was now also hers. She felt she shared it with her mother. She might never fully come to terms with her mother's death but, by working on the same pieces, she'd found some kind of acceptance for what had happened. She stood by the door, looking around, waiting for the familiar feelings to overwhelm her. But they didn't come. They were there, she knew, still lurking at the back of her mind, but she could control them, they didn't swamp her like they had before.

She looked across to the window seat but she wasn't tempted to retreat there like she'd always done. This time she walked over to the plan chest that stood behind her mother's desk and rummaged through it until she found what she was looking for. She withdrew the painting and placed it on the desk and smiled. Then she took the carefully folded sketch she'd tucked into her jacket pocket and smoothed it out on top of the painting. She'd gotten it right. She'd remembered every detail.

With her finger she traced around the lines of the joined initials of her mother's and her name, entwined together. Her mother had been working on the design before she'd separated from her father. A kielo—lily of the valley—the Finnish national flower which her father had bought her mother every day until they'd grown apart. Stylistically it was simple—the delicate cluster of white blossoms shaped like tiny bells wrought from platinum and gold, complementing and highlighting the diamonds Taina had chosen for it.

She felt closer to her mother than she'd done since she'd died, standing alone in her studio. Working on the initial drawings her mother had left behind, continuing the thought and flow of the design to its natural conclusion, she felt a connection with her spirit, understanding her mother's aim, where the unfinished lines should go. She realized that, if it weren't for Daidan, forcing her to work on the collection, she'd always have avoided it. And she'd never have made that connection with her mother.

After a while Taina held the sketch up to the light as she tried to figure out if she'd got the detailing right. Narrowing her eyes, she inspected the placement of the diamonds and smiled slowly, nodding to herself as she scanned outward to the platinum settings and further to the span of platinum and gold pieces that held it in place. They looked as fragile as gossamer. But they'd be as strong as the diamonds itself. The stylistic influence of her mother was there, but there was something of her, too.

Taina set to work again. The minutes drifted by until she lost track of the time she'd spent there. It was only when the room dimmed that she blinked and looked around. The sky had clouded over and the light had changed in the room. But it wasn't that that had disturbed her. She could distinctly hear someone moving around downstairs. She froze and her mind immediately returned to the encounter earlier with the Russians in the hotel. She must have forgotten to secure the alarm. She looked around, remembering with a paralyzing fear another time she'd been trapped in a room at the top of a flight of stairs with no way out. She couldn't let that happen again.

She stepped quietly, avoiding the creaky floorboards, to where the tools were. She picked up a small sharp hammer used for piercing metal and walked behind the door and raised the hammer. This time she'd defend herself.

The door swung open and nearly banged into her. "Taina!" Daidan's voice echoed around the space. "Taina!" he called again and she could hear the fear in his voice.

"Daidan!"

He swung around. "Thank God, I've found you. My men went to the wrong wharf. Given your previous reaction, I didn't imagine you'd come here. Anyway, what the hell were you doing behind the door?"

"Protecting myself," she said with a rueful smile. "I thought you were an intruder."

"I could well have been. It's not safe for you to be here on your own."

"You're obsessed with the idea that someone's after me. It has to stop, Daidan. Now. I can't live like this."

But Daidan didn't answer. Instead, he stalked over to the window and peered out, being careful to hide behind the curtain so no one could see him. "Come here, Taina. Look out here. What do you see?"

Puzzled, she did as he suggested and came up beside him and looked out. The beautiful buildings framed the trees in the park below, above which a cloudy sky held in the heat. There were more people walking around now, some of whom were tourists taking photographs. "It looks like normal. What am I meant to be looking at?"

"Down there, partly concealed by the trees."

Her sweeping gaze stopped. There were two people smoking in a studied, nonchalant way. They glanced nervously toward the building from time to time. She shrugged. "So? They could be anybody." But even as she spoke she felt uneasy. She recognized one of the men. He'd been in the hotel with the Russian group.

"They're not anybody, Taina. They're *Solntsevskaya Bratva*, the Russian mafia. They're part of the Kuzmich family who own the Chukotka mine."

"Kuzmich?" Then suddenly she remembered when she'd seen the man in the hotel. It must have been years before when he'd met with her father. She walked quickly away from the window. "Christ!" She sat down at the desk and held her head in her hands. "Christ," she repeated. Then she shook her head. "But they have interests in businesses in Helsinki—probably here in Katajanokka for all I know."

"Yes, they have business interests and our business threatens theirs. Our new safety measures have made us popular with buyers and we've taken some of their market share. It's also made their workers more demanding. Which does not make them very happy, to put it mildly." He turned away from the window and turned to look at her. "Have you any idea what these people are capable of?"

She shook her head. "You're exaggerating. Surely all that stuff is made up by the media."

"No, it's not. You've lived too long in a secluded world. It's my fault. I didn't want to worry you and protected you too much. It's time you learned what we're up against."

Daidan stood by the desk, hands thrust in his pockets while he spoke in short clipped sentences, describing in painfully clear language what exactly the Kuzmich family had been accused of doing over the past year, and what his contacts knew they'd done but which couldn't be proven.

At the end of the tirade, Taina shook her head, devastated by the risk she'd just run. "I had no idea."

"And then there's Sahmir's connection."

"What connection? What on earth has Sahmir to do with the Kuzmich family?"

"Yes, well, I probably shouldn't have kept you in the dark about this, either. But I didn't want to worry you. Sahmir's wife, Rory, got caught up in some bad business with Vadim Kuzmich, the son who died last year. He'd won Rory's estate from her father in a gambling session, and then decided he wanted Rory too. If it hadn't been for Sahmir he'd have had her too. It's another point of contention between our family and theirs. Another reason to get back at us. Another reason why I thought they might try to target you."

"I'm sorry. I thought you…" She trailed off. She couldn't bring herself to voice her doubts which seemed too stupid now, so disloyal, so naïve.

"You thought I was controlling you because that's how I wished you to be—under my control." He shook his head. "Despite what it looks like, I've never wanted that. If I had, don't you think I'd have gone looking for you after you left? No, I didn't do that because I believed you needed time and space, time to grow up, time to realize that our love for each other would overcome everything. You think I'm controlling? My dear Taina, I'm not controlling enough, otherwise you'd never have left me, and I'd not have let you slip through my fingers on the island this morning."

She pressed her lips in regret and nodded. "I'm sorry."

He shrugged. "Nothing bad happened."

"Should we leave, now? Is it safe?"

"It's safe. What you didn't see is my men who are watching over them."

"How long are we going to have this threat hanging over us?"

"Just until the launch. My sources tell me that it's the launch they see as easiest pickings. We'll have our biggest, most important clients all in one place. If the *Solntsevskaya Bratva* can disrupt it in some way, then the whole thing could work against us."

"Should we postpone it? Move it to a different location?"

"Any changes we make now will only play into their hands. Rumors will begin which we won't be able to stop. Plus what other location is there that we can secure as effectively as the island? There is none. No, the date and place of the launch stays. We'll ride it out until then."

"And after that?"

"After that we'll be in a stronger position to negotiate. We'll come to an agreement with them—there's no other way —but it'll be on my terms."

She nodded and fingered through her drawings absently. He came up behind her and placed his hands on her shoulders, kneading them gently. "Don't worry. Everything's under control. No one will get to you. I should have told you before but I thought it'd scare you away."

"It does scare me, but"—she twisted around to look at him—"I'm not going anywhere. I'm not running anymore."

"Good." He dropped a kiss on her forehead. "now show me what you've been working on."

She pushed the papers over to him. "I'm happy with how it's turned out. What do you think?"

"It's beautiful." He leaned over and traced his finger over its lines. "You've blended both your's and your mother's style to create one all of its own. It's too late to make the piece for the launch, but we can use the designs themselves to showcase what's coming in the future. Whet people's appetite for

119

next year's collection. Show people what a great future awaits the company."

She grinned to herself but didn't say anything, just turned her head to one side so he wouldn't see how much his words meant to her.

"Taina? Don't you agree?"

She nodded her head in agreement but still couldn't say anything.

"Taina!" He dipped his head and lifted her chin. "My Taina, tell me what you're thinking."

The grin broke into a laugh, this time enjoying the note of possession in his words. "I'm thinking we both have a great future ahead of us." She rose and kissed him. "Now, let's get back to the island and sort out this launch. The sooner it's over the sooner we can be free of all of this and get on with our lives."

IN THE EARLY hours of the morning Taina cried out loud and awoke with a start. She sat up, heart pounding, her night slip sticking to her back. She turned on the light and looked around. There was no one there. She was alone. She took a deep breath and exhaled heavily. Of course she was alone. Daidan rarely slept more than a few hours and the man in her nightmares was far away and she wouldn't be seeing him again. She'd always made sure they were never in the same city, even the same country, at the same time. She was safe.

"Taina?" Daidan called as she heard his footsteps coming toward the bedroom. He burst open the door, hair wet, wearing nothing but a towel around his waist. "Taina, are you okay?"

"I'm fine." She looked him up and down and felt the thrill she always felt at the sight of him. "Don't you ever sleep?"

"Rarely. I thought I'd shower in the other bathroom so I didn't disturb you and then get on with some work. Are you okay? I thought I heard you cry out."

She pushed her hair of her face and half-turned away, not wanting him to see her distress. "Just a nightmare. I have them from time to time."

"You had another one on the plane. You never used to have nightmares."

She glanced at him. "Yeah, well, times have changed." She walked over to the window and opened the curtains, letting in the half-light of midnight. The scented air from the garden below mingled with the salty edge of the sea. She turned back to him and smiled. "But when you're beside me I don't have them. I feel a lot of things when you're with me, but they don't include fear. Are you going to stay a little while? Would you like a drink? A whiskey?" She went to the dresser and held up the decanter.

"Why not?" He walked to the window where the castle ruins rose from the dark into the inky dusk sky. "Only a few days away now."

She brought over two drinks and handed him one. "Will you be relieved when it's over?"

"Oh, yes. I'm not good at all this marketing like you are."

She shrugged, looked at the whiskey which suddenly didn't appeal, and set it on the table. "I don't know if I'm good at it. Just seems people are interested in me because I'm a member of the Mustonen family."

"You're rich, you're beautiful and you're charming. That makes you a marketer's dream."

She narrowed her eyes. "And is that why you're interested in me?"

"I know plenty of rich, beautiful, charming women, but I've only ever wanted to make one my wife. And that's you."

He sat further back in his chair and swirled his whiskey thoughtfully.

"I never did understand why. To begin with I thought it was my connections and then… and then, after I fell in love with you, I couldn't bear to think it was that. I persuaded myself that, out of some miracle, you loved me. Me!" She shook her head. "And then, after the wedding, which we rushed to get organized before Papa died, but he didn't even last till then, the lawyer spoke about his will and wishes and I thought, how could I have been so stupid? I was right the first time."

He rose and came over to her by the window and extended his hand to hers. She reached out for him, watching his fingers curl around hers, not able to look up at him, all her thought and sensation wrapped up in the coming together of their hands. Something that happened all the time between people, whether they were known to each other or not. And yet this act seemed more intimate than any of the other intimacy they'd had recently.

"Taina, look at me."

She swallowed and looked up at him as he spoke gently. "I'm so sorry. When your father and I discussed my marriage to you and I realized he was all for it, I couldn't believe my luck. I'd always wanted a family of my own and as it happened that's what he wanted. He was afraid for you, afraid you'd be taken advantage of, and he knew he was dying. He wanted to see you settled; he wanted both the company and *you* in good hands. And I am good hands, you know, Taina."

She took his hands in hers and inspected them, her lips twisting into a wry smile. She looked up at him from beneath lowered lids. "I do know." She kissed his palms before he held her face and kissed her tenderly. She melted deep inside, under the gentle command of his mouth. She had no thought, no feeling, that wasn't connected to the movement of his lips against hers, the slide of his tongue against hers. Delicious shivers of sensual anticipation coursed through her body. She pulled away. "I do know, but maybe you should show me just how good your hands are?" She backed toward the bed.

He narrowed his eyes in mock anger. "You, *habibti*, are a tease."

She cocked an eyebrow, her eyes checking the movement beneath his towel. "A tease? Someone who has no intention of following up? Is that what you think me?"

"Taina," he said with a husky, dangerously low voice, as he advanced on her.

"Well, there's only one way to find out," she said, continuing to step back until the bed stopped her movement. Before she could side-step it, he grabbed her and proceeded to show her in no uncertain terms that "following up" was exactly what they'd be doing, and just how good his hands were.

LONG AFTER SHE'D fallen asleep, Daidan continued to hold Taina. He softly stroked her clear forehead and gently kissed her head, mussing her blond hair with his lips. She shifted every now and then and whimpered a little. He'd stroke her face, massage away the frown on her brow and she'd sigh, roll into his body, brush her lips against his chest and fall asleep once more.

How on earth had this woman whom he loved so dearly ended up pregnant by another man? It was so unlike her to have a casual relationship. Taina wasn't casual about anything. The thought of her with another man made him sick to his stomach, but he didn't stop caressing her. He might never know exactly what had happened but it wouldn't stop him from being with her, from loving her. It also wouldn't stop the hurt and frustration which refused to leave him.

Hours later, he eased his arms from beneath her and rose. He'd go to his study and work, just as he had done while she was away. At least that diverted his mind for a little while.

TAINA AWOKE with a start once more. Two nightmares in one night. Wouldn't it ever end? She blinked against the bright sun that was streaming into her bedroom. There was no sign of Daidan. His place in the bed was cold. Out of all the things he'd said, he'd not once said that he'd forgiven her. She doubted he ever would. No, he must have left as soon as they'd make love and she'd drifted off to sleep.

She sat on the edge of her bed, trying to repel the vestiges of her nightmare, her feelings of helplessness. She rubbed her wrists, as if she could feel the ropes chafing them, just as they had done. She doubted the feelings of humiliation and anguish would ever leave her. She stood up and pulled her hair back into a tight ponytail. She'd shower, she'd get herself together like she had every day since. She'd tidy everything up so that it was as if it had never happened. Just like she always did. Nothing more for Daidan to know about.

It'd be better for Daidan to believe the child was a product of some temporary liaison rather than the truth. Because she couldn't trust Daidan's passionate nature not to take the law into his own hands.

CHAPTER 9

*T*aina pressed save on the computer and rolled her shoulders, checking to make sure the finishing touches to the presentation had been saved properly. Then she forwarded it to Daidan's computer. The flickering light blinked off and she ejected the memory stick. At last! Done!

Feeling as if a weight had been lifted from her shoulders, she pocketed the memory stick and rose from the desk where she'd been working for the past four hours, since three in the morning. Now it was morning and she could hear staff at work in the office with Daidan.

She went into the dining room where breakfast was laid out for anyone who wanted it. Her stomach turned at the smell of the cooked food and she picked up a croissant and glass of mineral water instead. She took a bite of the croissant, pulled a face and then left the rest, focusing on the water. Strange, she felt a little queasy. Too much work and not enough sleep.

She wandered into the living room with her glass of water. She sat down on the leather couch and suddenly remembered sitting on the same couch when she'd first come to see Daidan with her proposition in spring. Three months ago. An age ago. But now it was midsummer and the open windows let in warm morning air, not snow. And that wasn't the only thing that had changed. She'd been afraid that this house would feel like a prison to her, as it had been when she'd grown up here. But to her amazement it hadn't. And that was down to Daidan. He'd kept her safe here on the island but he hadn't kept her a prisoner. He'd been right—it had been safest for them to stay on the island until the launch, and emotionally and intellectually she'd been free.

During the day she'd worked on the designs for the next collection, building on and incorporating her mother's designs, bringing them up to the minute with her own spin. And at night Daidan had set her free, physically and emotionally. They'd come to know each other more intimately than ever before and she'd sensed a shift in him. He didn't talk about her past any more. It seemed he'd come to some kind of decision to not let any jealousy, any sadness about what had happened to her to interfere with their future. And for that she was thankful.

She finished her water and walked along the corridor, lined with priceless artworks, to the office. His door was open wide and he along with two others were seated around the table, already going over the arrangements, down to the most minute detail.

"Taina." He smiled. "Come and join us. We were just going through the last minute changes to the guest list."

Taina hardly registered his comment, more struck by the warmth of his tone, so different to how it had been just weeks ago. "No, that's fine. I've seen an earlier one. I guess there are no major changes to it?"

"Just a few tweaks."

"Then I'll let you get on. I'm only here to make sure you have the latest presentation materials." She waved the memory stick. "I've already forwarded it to you, but I'll just leave this here." She looked down at a dozen other similar memory sticks. "Hm, maybe I'll just make this final one a bit more distinctive."

She returned a few minutes later with the palest pink nail varnish and proceeded to paint the outline of a flower onto the stick. She held it up to him.

"A kielo, if I'm not mistaken," he said.

"Now you can't get it confused."

She waved goodbye and left them to it. She returned to her bedroom, drew the curtains closed and lay on her bed and was instantly asleep.

"TAINA." Daidan's voice swept like a wave into her dreams, rousing her gently. He kissed her and her eyes fluttered open. "You've been asleep all day." He frowned. "Are you feeling well?"

She stretched like a cat. "I'm feeling better now."

"Dinner is served on the terrace."

She knelt on the bed and put her arms around him and nuzzled his neck. "Hm, I think I'm in the mood for something pre-dinner."

He grunted. "I take it you're not meaning an aperitif."

"You take it right," she said as she unbuttoned his shirt.

"IT'S JUST AS WELL it's a cold platter," Taina commented as she lifted the lids on the trays a few hours later.

Daidan sat down opposite her. His face was shadowed in the twilight that counted as night in midsummer. It would last only a few hours before morning broke again in the early hours. An owl hooted from the trees and the water lapped against the small pebbly beach under the deck. "If it had been a hot dinner, I'd have dealt with you in a much shorter time."

She threw a bread roll at him and annoyingly he caught it and ate it. She sat back and picked at her food. "It's so beautiful out here. Some of my favorite memories of Mama are of her sitting out here in the summer evenings, just dreaming, listening to music, talking in a low voice to Papa. When it was time for me to go to bed, I'd creep to the open window so I could hear them. And I'd go to sleep to the sound of their voices, their soft laughter and the murmur of the water." She sighed.

"Special memories."

"Yes. White nights. Mama had white-blond hair and loved beautiful clothes. Clothes that floated in the air, light as gossamer. They suited her personality. Magical, ethereal. Not quite at ease in the real world."

Daidan reached for her hand. "I'm sorry."

"Not as sorry as I am. I miss her. I would have liked her company for longer. Liked to get to know her better. Liked to laugh with her like Papa used to do here, on the terrace."

"You can do that with your own children."

"Yes." The thought made her happy. She suddenly remembered her queasiness. Could she be? After dinner she'd check. It seemed hard to believe that she'd fall pregnant quite so easily, but it wasn't out of the question.

"And what, Taina, are you grinning at?"

"Just a thought."

"We'll have children, Taina. Just be patient."

She didn't say anything. Just looked up at him and smiled.

TAINA PACED up and down the bathroom as she waited for the pregnancy test to perform its magic. She'd bought some tests after their first lovemaking, but they hadn't all been used since she'd gotten her period. Though it had been lighter than usual... Of course she couldn't be pregnant. When had anything she'd wanted so badly come to pass? Patient? She'd only been patient up till the moment she realized she could be pregnant and then each minute until they went to bed had seemed like an hour.

She stopped at the basin upon which the pregnancy test stick was balanced. Nothing. She sucked in a harsh breath. Ridiculous. Her aching need to be pregnant had lessened with each passing week with Daidan. She still wanted children, but not with the same obsessional drive. What had been a sharp pain, motivating everything she did, had turned into a dull ache she could live with, which didn't drive everything she said and did. She was with Daidan and, miraculously, they were happy. But then this... And now it seemed her whole life depended on whether that thin blue strip appeared on the test stick.

She paced again to the window, and looked out over the rear of the property. The land sloped down to the sea, silver under the crescent moon. The eerie light seemed to emphasize the feeling that she was standing on a precipice—change lay before her like a vast unknowing and unknowable plain. After tomorrow—the day of the launch—everything would change again.

A distant owl hooted, declaring its territory. She felt a buzz of excitement as she realized a good minute must have passed. She had to look back at the stick. Steeling herself for a disappointment, she looked straight ahead and caught sight of herself in the mirror. She looked pale, her eyes unnaturally bright. She shook her head at the sight of herself because she'd also changed. Her short, choppy hairstyle had become neglected as she'd focused on her work. The makeup that she'd always taken such trouble to apply had been forgotten about as she'd been in such a rush to get to the studio and get back to work. Her skin was clear and glowing. She'd never looked more natural and she'd never felt more happy. Whatever was on the stick, she'd be happy, she decided. She would.

She looked down. There was no thin narrow strip of blue that she'd hoped for so much. She looked again, tilting it to the light. But it made no difference. She wasn't pregnant. She blinked and stared at it for a few seconds more before she rose and walled off the hope. She gripped the basin and dropped her head as she suddenly felt faint. She splashed cold water onto her face and blotted it away with a soft white towel. Must have been something she'd eaten.

THE SOUND CHECKS were going on at the castle. The stage, seating, and lighting were all in place and the orchestra and singers were having a rehearsal.

Taina had been enjoying the sun and sketching the castle and various flowers as Daidan came and took a seat beside her. "How's it sounding?"

"Fantastic."

"Everything else okay?"

"Hope so."

"Don't sound so worried. It'll all be fine. Everything's arranged. Everything's in place."

"Yeah, I know. Most things anyway. There's been a few more changes."

She frowned. "What?"

"Come on, I'll show you."

She took his hand and rose. She suddenly felt faint and staggered.

Daidan held her tight. "What's the matter?"

She swayed. "I feel… I feel…"

And then she fainted in his arms.

"IT'S NOT NECESSARY," Taina hissed at Daidan as they waited for the doctor to appear. She'd already given blood and a urine sample. "We shouldn't be away from the island. It's a risk we don't need to take."

"It's a greater risk not knowing why you fainted." Daidan rose. "Doctor, good of you to see us at such short notice."

Dr Linna smiled at Taina. "I've been seeing Taina since she was a young girl. Good to see you again, my dear." He sat down. "Now, what's the problem?"

"It's just the heat. I was working in the sun and then walking through the castle grounds."

"Have you fainted before in the heat?"

She shook her head.

"Well then, it's worth investigating." Without further comment the doctor went about doing routine checks.

At the end he set aside his stethoscope and took a folder of papers from the nurse who stopped by. Minutes passed as the doctor read through the results of the tests.

"So?" asked a worried Daidan.

The doctor smiled from one to the other. "Nothing to be concerned about. All very natural for someone who's pregnant. Less than three months, I suspect."

Taina jumped up and shook her head. "No, I can't be. I've had my period and I've done a pregnancy test—"

"You have?" asked Daidan in surprise.

She nodded. "But it was negative."

"Sometimes those tests are unreliable. Your blood test confirms it."

Taina paced the room. "No, I'm sure it's just the heat."

"Is this something you weren't expecting?" the doctor asked.

"Perhaps not yet," said Daidan, looking anxiously at Taina. "But we *have* decided to have children." The doctor and Daidan both looked at Taina. "Taina? What is it?"

Taina couldn't answer. Shocked by the news after she'd persuaded herself she wasn't pregnant, out of the blue she felt floored, unable to believe it. She gripped the window sill and pushed open the window gulping in the fresh air. She shook her head.

"Hm, sometimes it helps to see something a bit more concrete than a blue line. I'll get the scanning equipment in and that should make things a bit clearer for you."

Within minutes the equipment had been wheeled in and Taina lay with one arm behind her head looking at the screen as the doctor ran the scanner over her stomach. "There's nothing there, doctor. I told you." She turned her head to Daidan whose eyes were firmly on the screen. "Daidan, this is a waste of time. Let's go home." Then Daidan's eyes opened wide. "There's nothing there, I tell you," she insisted.

He nodded. "Look, Taina, just look."

She didn't dare. Fear seized her and she continued to look at Daidan. She felt herself beginning to shake. "I can't," she whispered. "I can't." She wiped away a tear as it tracked down her face, but more followed. "I can't," she repeated, her voice suddenly hoarse.

Daidan squeezed her hand. "Yes, you can. Look, Taina, look."

Slowly Taina turned to face the screen. There the flowing, moving contours suddenly stopped to reveal a tiny form. She didn't have to see its shape, its features, to know what she was seeing. She'd seen the same thing a year ago—larger, more clear, but the same and she remembered how she'd felt with vivid clarity. How she'd hated the vision, how she'd wished it dead.

With tears streaming down her face, she looked up at Daidan and shook her head. "I wished her dead," she whispered between sobs.

He took hold of her, his gaze no longer on the screen, but on Taina. "What? What did you say?"

"I wished her dead." She gulped. "When I saw her like this. It was my fault. My fault that she died."

"What are you talking about?"

But Taina had to get out of there and pushed away the scanner, the other stuff and stood up, pulling down her top. "I've got to go, Daidan. I have to go, now."

The doctor frowned and spoke briefly to Daidan. Taina couldn't hear what he said because she was out of there. Pushing open the door, as if in slow motion, walking outside, breathing deeply, trying to control the grief that threatened to overwhelm her.

She got in the car and waited, gasping as she tried to catch her breath between sobs. Then Daidan got in the driver's seat and watched her. "Here, the doctor gave me some pills to help you calm down." She swallowed them and rested her head back against the seat with a shuddering breath.

"I'm okay. Let's go home."

He nodded and drove to the port where he helped her onto the waiting boat. It was only when they'd reached the island, that the staff had been dismissed, that there was only the two of them, that he asked her the question she'd been waiting for.

"Why did you wish your child to be dead, Taina? Why? I don't understand."

She was lulled by the pills the doctor had given her. She felt dreamy, unreal. She rolled her head on the back of the sofa to face him. His face seemed to come into and out of focus. But his words hammered home with deathly clarity.

"Why?"

"Because…" She closed her eyes. It could have been for a second or minutes. But when she opened them he was still looking at her intently. She struggled to sit up and took a drink of water that had miraculously appeared beside her. "Because I didn't want her."

"Why?"

The word came to her like a breath of wind, barely felt, hardly heard. "Why? Because she reminded me of something I wanted to forget."

This time there was no prompting question. But she heard his unspoken question nevertheless, like it was a command she wanted to answer.

She sighed and lay back again, looking straight at one of her mother's paintings. "How she began. The violence of her… conception…" She closed her eyes again and when she opened them, again she wondered if she'd been asleep for moments only or minutes. "Or not so violent. Apparently the drug I'd been given in my drink had knocked me out so that I could see and feel everything, I just couldn't respond. So no violence required. Just…" She rubbed her wrists but didn't elaborate. There was a long pause. "I was raped, Daidan. My child was a product of a rape. That is why I wished her dead."

DAIDAN DIDN'T THINK he'd ever forget the look of numb grief on her face. And he'd certainly never forget how *he* felt. No matter that he didn't let it surface. There was time later for that. But he knew what he needed to do. He simply held her. She didn't cry again, the drugs had dulled her emotional pain. But he knew it would be different the next day.

Lulled by his reassurance and the numbing of the sedative

she soon fell asleep. He carried her over to the bed. Deliberately and carefully he pulled off her shoes and brought the covers over her. Then he stood back and looked at her and his heart ached. He'd wanted to protect Taina from the whole world. He'd wanted her never to be hurt. He'd wanted to always care for her, to love her with a simple, strong love that would survive everything. Instead, he'd driven her away, into the arms of a rapist. And it had been his fault.

As he closed the curtains and quietly left the room, he thought he'd never forgive himself. There was only one thing he wanted to know now. Who was the man who'd raped the woman he loved?

CHAPTER 10

*N*ext morning Daidan was nowhere to be found. She'd rung the office in the city. Nothing. She'd contacted his people who were working at the castle. Nothing. And she needed to find him because now that the sedatives the doctor had given Taina had worn off, she could think clearly. The shock of pregnancy had disappeared leaving only happiness and relief. But, at that moment another fear was uppermost in her mind—had she really told Daidan everything, or had she dreamed it?

She paced the length of the lounge, trying to remember, trying to pinpoint her words to something concrete, something real. Then she stopped pacing as she caught sight of her mother's painting and she suddenly remembered. She'd been looking at it when the words had formed on her lips—violence…rape. Looking at the same painting now, she had a sudden vision of Daidan's shattered expression. She clasped her hands to her head and gasped. She hadn't dreamed any of it. She'd told him. And he wasn't anywhere to be found. Where the hell was he?

The phone went and she jumped. "Yes?" But it was just

someone reporting somewhere else that Daidan *hadn't* been seen.

She grunted in frustration, threw down the phone onto the sofa and went down the corridor to her room to get her sunglasses. As she passed Daidan's dressing room she stopped. Maybe there would be clues in there? Besides, she desperately wanted to feel close to him.

She opened the door. Inside the room was orderly. Everything was in its place—shirts pressed and hung with clinical precision, shoes polished and stored on racks. She walked in and stopped suddenly. Why did she feel so strange? And then she closed her eyes as it came to her. It had been her father's dressing room and the only time she'd been inside was when he hadn't been around and she'd been secretly trying to find something of her mother's—anything that would make a connection she so desperately craved. She hadn't found anything then. And it didn't look like she'd find any clues to help her locate Daidan now. Because, like her father, Daidan kept everything immaculate. Or almost everything, she thought as she walked to the tallboy, on which a few personal objects were displayed.

She picked up a small figurine she'd made. Her tutor had been world class; she hadn't been. She smiled as she remembered her father's pride, and placed it back in position. Why had Daidan kept it? Then she saw that he'd moved a family photograph that had been there in her father's time—moved it to make way for another photograph—one of her and Daidan, shortly before they were married. The happiness that shone from their eyes as they embraced and smiled for the camera brought tears to her eyes. How had it all disappeared in such a short space of time? She'd do anything to see Daidan happy again.

But she knew he'd be far from happy at this moment. She could almost sense his feelings of anger and frustration. But how else would he react? He'd want to know who'd raped her and why she hadn't reported it. She could lie and tell him she didn't know the person but she didn't want any more lies. That only left the truth. But she couldn't do that yet, not before the launch. Nothing must go wrong with that. Because the truth could destroy all the work and hopes and dreams Daidan had for himself, for them, and for their future together.

She paced over to the windows and opened them to let the sea breeze cool her agitation. Think, Taina, think! He couldn't have vanished into thin air. She stepped outside onto the deck and walked down the steps and turned away from the sea, toward the rear of the house where the gardens descended into a thick copse of trees. The boat was still here. He must be on the island, just not with anyone. And she knew the island better than anyone. If he *was* here, she'd find him.

It wasn't until she reached the edge of the woods that she heard the sound of someone chopping wood. Strange. It was still summer. The handyman usually chopped the wood for the fire later in the year. She shrugged and was about to take a path that led around the water's edge when she stopped once more. There was something in the sound of the chopping—something rhythmic and savage—that made her hesitate. Then she closed her eyes as she realized she was listening to a man venting his grief in the only way he could. She turned and ran down the path into the woods towards the sound.

DAIDAN SWUNG THE AXE OVERHEAD, held it for an instant, relishing the feel of his muscles pumped and strong before bringing it down with a reverberating thud onto the block of wood, splitting it cleanly in two. He replaced half onto the block and once more swung the axe up over his head. Sweat trickled down his face, stinging his eyes, blinding him as he let it fall once more with a savage blow. He repeated the action with a rhythm that obscured the need to feel. The wood flew in different directions, piling up wherever it landed. All he wanted to do was use his strength against the wood. All he wanted to do was dull the pain.

"Daidan!" Taina's voice drifted down through the trees. He hesitated, the axe high over his head, and then let it swing down.

"Daidan," the voice repeated, closer now. He glanced up to see her running down the dry track between the trees.

"Daidan!" she shouted, nearer now. He could hardly bear to see her. The pain dug in, deep inside.

He raised the axe once more before slamming the blade into another tree stump. He turned around, chest heaving, hands on hips. Even seeing her there, her delicate beauty a sharp contrast to the chaos of cut logs and his sweaty, grimy body, emphasized her vulnerability, underscored how much he'd failed her.

He tried to smile at her reassuringly but reckoned he'd failed because she looked anything but reassured. He might be suffering but it was Taina who'd suffered most. "I thought you'd still be sleeping," he said, in as calm a tone as he could manage.

"No, I've been looking for you."

"You okay?" he asked.

She nodded. "Fine. More than fine about the baby." She rubbed her stomach gently. "I guess it was just the shock, the memory of my last scan… it just got to me. But I want to know how you are."

"Fine," he muttered between gritted teeth before he turned away and pulled the axe blade from the log. He placed another log on the chopping block. But before his grip could tighten on the axe, Taina came and rested her hand on his arm.

"Daidan, I'm so sorry."

He focused on his hands, flexing around the axe handle. "Who was he, Taina? Did you know him?"

Taina twisted her lips and turned away. She did know him. He could see it.

"Right. Who was he?"

"I can't tell you."

"Can't or won't?"

"Won't. Not now. Not yet."

"Then when?"

"When you're less angry."

He grunted. She was right. He'd never been so angry, or felt so helpless in his whole life. If he knew who had hurt her he'd ignore the launch, ignore everything until he could pummel the man who'd caused her such pain. His much-vaunted control had disappeared in an instant with her words. He took a deep breath and then looked up at her. "Why don't you go back to the house? You could get hurt here." It was taking all his will power to remain calm.

"No. Come with me, now."

"What's the point when you won't tell me what I need to know?"

"I want *you* to talk to *me*. Tell me how you feel, what you're thinking. We *have* to be able to talk to each other about this."

"I thought you claimed you knew how I felt—angry."

"That much I can guess. You're angry with me for keeping secrets from you."

He grunted. "Correct. But that's not all."

"And for running away on our wedding day."

"No, I'm not angry with you for that. You ran because

your father and I had driven you away. Try again." He could feel his control slipping.

"Well, if not for that, you're angry that I didn't return."

"No! Wrong again. Hurt maybe, but not angry. Not at you." His voice was growing louder but he seemed unable to stop it.

She shook her head, bewildered. "Hurt that I didn't tell you what happened?"

He took the hand that held his and gripped it in his before dropping it by her side. "Just leave it, Taina. You've done nothing wrong apart from being so damned secretive. But even that I can sort of understand. You were afraid how I'd react, afraid I'd take the law into my own hands."

"Wouldn't you?"

He began picking up logs and tossing them toward the pile. Taina stepped out the way. "Probably," he answered at last. He continued in silence... one, two, three logs. Then walked and picked up some more without looking around. Five minutes must have passed before he stopped, sighed, dropped his head and wondered what the hell he had to do to make Taina leave.

"I'm not going until you talk to me," the quiet but firm voice said.

He walked over to where he'd tossed his shirt and pulled it on, without looking at her. He took another deep breath and then turned to her. "So... what do you want me to say?"

"So if you're not angry with me, who are you angry with?"

He tugged his shirt together and began buttoning it up. "Me, of course! I'm furious with *me*. I failed you."

Taina ran to him, slipped her arms under his shirt and pressed her cheek against his bare chest. "You didn't fail me, you stupid man. You didn't. How could you fail me when you weren't there? It was all my stupid fault. I ran away because I felt betrayed by you and Papa. I should have stayed and forced you to understand. Instead I went from one resort, one city to another, a child trying to mix in an adult world. I was unprepared… naïve. I didn't read the signs, wasn't aware of the undercurrents. I'd been too protected all my life to understand what was going to happen."

He felt his heart would break as he looked down at her and pictured her trying to fit into the superficial world of the rich and famous, imagined her being taken advantage of.

"I'm angry because I failed you. I should have been there. I didn't follow you—probably a combination of my stupid pride and the realization that your reaction was quite reasonable when seen from your perspective—and I should have. And we've both paid the price." He looked down to find his hands had moved of their own volition and were stroking her upper arms. "Why didn't you tell me, Taina? Why?" He didn't recognize his voice—made hoarse by the pain he was trying so desperately to rid himself of.

"Because I was scared." A tear trickled down her cheek.

"Why? Scared of what? Surely I'm not worse than a rapist?"

Her breath hitched as she tried to calm herself, tried to stop the tears. "Of course not." She closed her eyes as if trying to put herself back in that time. "To begin with"—she opened her eyes, looking stronger now—"I thought it must have been my fault somehow. I believed what… he said to me. And then, later, I thought it's best forgotten. That's what we always did in my house when I was growing up. If something nasty happened, like finding Mama drunk on the sofa, it was covered up. Next morning back to normal, nothing said. So that's what I thought I'd do." She fought back more tears. "And then my body changed and I ignored it for too long. Abortion was no longer an option by the time I was forced by my doctor to face the fact that I was pregnant. So I went away. To the Far East. Singapore."

"You left no trace."

"No. I have access to my own funds from my mother's inheritance. I used those. Kept quiet. Told no one except the hospital and waited. Day in, day out, watching my body change. And hating it. Just waiting for the day when my body would expel the invader, and it could be adopted out, and I could get on with my life."

"You saw no one you knew? You had no one with you?"

"Just paid help." She half-laughed. "Much like my time growing up. It wasn't so strange for me." She looked up at him with those violet eyes. "But being pregnant was. I hated it."

"So what happened?"

"The usual. On the due date I had the baby. A difficult birth. You wouldn't have recognized me—cursing and swearing and a total mess. And then..."

There was a long pause and he tilted her chin so the dappled light moved upon her creamy skin. "And then she arrived. I called her Mimi, after my mother. I wasn't even going to name her but she arrived, and some nurse who didn't realize I wanted to adopt the child out placed her to my breast, and Mimi looked up at me and stared at me. Apparently not many babies do that. But Mimi did. It was like she was saying 'Don't you dare let me go. Don't you dare'. One of the nurses said she had the eyes of an old soul."

"What did she mean?"

"Like she'd already lived, I suppose. She certainly had knowing eyes, like she could see right into you. There was no way I was going to let her go. It wasn't even a decision I had to think through. I knew it viscerally. Like she'd planted the thought in my head and my whole being agreed. There was no question about it."

The memories must have taken over because Taina stopped talking and Daidan wove his hands through her hair and brought her against him. Just holding her, giving the only comfort he could, himself. There was no sound except for the birds in the trees around them and a distant sound of a motor boat out in the Gulf. It was all so familiar and yet felt different now. Like they'd turned a corner, like he was looking at everything with new eyes.

She looked up at him suddenly and tears were streaming down her face. "They told me there were complications. But she looked so perfect I didn't believe them at first."

"What kind of complications?"

"Mimi had a heart defect. I thought, I have money, we'll get it cured." She clamped her quivering lips together, but it didn't stop the tears from falling. "Turns out I couldn't. They let me take her back to my apartment for a few weeks at the end. I think I kidded myself that it was all okay, that the nurse was just there as a precaution. But I knew really. I knew. And she died in my arms."

Taina couldn't hold back the emotion any longer and lifted her head and let out a long howl that sent shivers down Daidan's spine. Then she pounded his chest with her fists and slumped against him and sobbed and sobbed as she should have sobbed all those months ago.

And he let her. He just held her, saying soothing things in Arabic that he'd forgotten he knew, things his nurse had said to him when he was a small child, angry and hurt by his lot in life. He tried to swallow down the lump in his throat but it wouldn't go. He tried to stop the tears from flowing but they wouldn't.

He said many things—soothing things, reassuring things, things that might help her—but none of them helped him. There was only one thing he couldn't ask, that he was desperate to know—*who was the bastard who raped you?*

Instead he helped Taina back to the house, supporting her

with his strength because that was all he could do, all he had to offer.

She walked to the window, looking out at God knew what.

"Are you okay? Would you like something? A drink? Coffee? Water?"

She shook her head. "Nothing."

"What can I do for you?" He swept his fingers helplessly through his hair. "How can I help you get over this? You've got to let me do something."

"You *are* helping me."

He shook his head. "How can I be? I've nothing to give you, nothing to say. You won't..." ...tell me his name, he was about to add before he stopped himself just in time. That wouldn't help her. But what else could he do? He'd been completely inept, completely incompetent at doing anything. All he had was his strength—mental and physical.

He took a soft throw from one of the leather chairs and took it to her, putting it around her shoulders but she put her hand on it and shook her head. "It's okay. I'm not an invalid. I've a little piece in my heart which will always be vulnerable, always a little broken, but since I've been back something's happened that I never expected."

"What's that?"

"I've grown stronger." She grimaced a little as if trying to think of words to express how she felt. "I'll tell you how it feels. You know when you hurt yourself, maybe strain your back through exercise or something? Then all the muscles tighten around it, trying to protect it, knowing it can't look after itself?" She smiled at him. It was like a watery sun after showers. "It's a bit like that. I'm stronger. And that's thanks to you. I came back here wanting another child to love, not able to bear the pain of Mimi's absence. But you gave me a connection to my past, to my family, to my country and land

and my art… and to you." She extended her hand to him. "And that's made me strong in a way I hadn't believed possible."

He took her hand and she seemed to reel him in to her. She ran her fingers over his cheeks and he closed his eyes, only opening them when she trailed her finger over his lips. "You are so beautiful, Daidan. I can't believe I walked away from you on our wedding day."

"You had every right to."

"Maybe. But I should have stayed. I should have made a scene—screamed at you, thrown things at you. Told you exactly what I thought of you and what you'd done."

He smiled. "I would have understood it better."

"Yes, our people, our cultures are so different. Us Finns are an introverted lot. I grew up with a family who was never open with their feelings or thoughts. It drove my mother to drink and my father to become obsessed with the company, with work, with diamonds. It drives the poison inside. I won't do that again. I'll always be open with you."

Again, the drive for him to ask the question that haunted him, framed itself in his mind, formed into teasing consonants in his mouth. His lips began to form the words but then she lifted herself up on tip-toe and kissed his mouth and the words were wiped out.

He swept his arms around her, pulling her to him, tasting her lips, her mouth, as if he were a starving man. All his frustrations and anger suddenly transformed into a desperate need to make love to this woman, hurt but strong—his wife.

The kiss deepened and she pressed her body against his, making it clear that she, too, wanted him. He put his hands beneath her bottom and lifted her up. Her legs curled around his hips as they continued to kiss. At last they pulled apart, breathless with need.

He pulled her to him, so her sex rubbed against his, showing her how much he wanted her.

"Take me, now," she whispered.

He put her down on the leather chaise that was bathed in light and began to take off her clothes. He took his time, relishing the signs that she needed him—as she tried to make him hurry, moving her body so sensuously in the flickering light from the leaves outside the window. He smiled when she grunted with frustration as he slowly stripped. Naked, he stood admiring her. It was only when she reached down and touched herself, opening herself for him to see how much she wanted him, that he moved. Lifting her legs until she was wrapped around him, he thrust into her, watching her eyes become heavy lidded but focusing on him. It was totally erotic.

And afterwards, with limbs tangled and their breathing returned to normal, as he caressed her stomach tenderly, did he suddenly realize that she was right. Taina was no longer a girl, but a woman—a strong woman.

She twisted in his arms. "What are you thinking about?"

"I need to know who it was. You knew who it was, didn't you? You knew the man who raped you."

She hesitated, pressing her lips together, uncertain what to do. But she'd told him things would change. She promised herself no more lies. She nodded.

"And you still won't tell me?"

"Not yet. I will. After…"

"After the launch?"

"Yes. After the launch I'll tell you."

"Because the person is connected to it?"

"Maybe. Please, leave it for now. I promise I will tell you. But you have to promise not to do anything."

"I can't promise that," he said quietly. "But I can promise I'll always love you."

147

She sat astride him and he knew that she was distracting him. And it was working. "Good." She moved her hands over him, playing with him, teasing him, until he forgot what he was thinking and surrendered to the movement of her hands, and then her body moving on him.

TAINA AWOKE to find the soft throw had been placed over her. She turned with a start. Daidan was dressed and sipping coffee and watching her. She sat up and yawned. "How long have I been asleep?"

"About an hour. Coffee?"

"Thank you." She sipped the coffee, the throw falling down to her waist, as did his eyes. He grinned. "So… are you going to sit there all day watching my breasts? Might get a tad boring."

"I'll never be bored by that. I could do it all day. Such perfect breasts."

She frowned. "Nothing's perfect, Daidan."

He grinned. "True. I think one might be a shade larger than the other."

She grabbed a cushion and threw it at him but he side-stepped it. "Thank you for considering my comfort but I won't be staying long."

She raised her eyebrows as she sipped her coffee. "Why? Where are you going?"

"I'm not going anywhere." He pointed out the window to the gulf. "See the boat out there?"

Taina looked at the launch that appeared to be heading their way. She pulled the throw around her and stood up. "Is someone coming?"

"Our team, Taina. The whole of our team will be arriving in, oh"—he glanced at his watch and looked up at her with a grin—"in approximately eight minutes."

148

Taina yelped and her coffee spilled as she ran from the room. "Bastard!"

DAIDAN SMILED to himself as he heard Taina running down the hall to their suite at the far end of the house. He watched the boat approach as he calmly finished his coffee. Taina was wrong about something. He still felt unable to help her, except in this one way. He could protect her from threat. He suspected one of the Russian contingent. They'd been both in Antigua and New York before at the same time she was there. He'd make sure they couldn't get anywhere near her before he discovered the rapist's identity and dealt with him. Only then could he and Taina move on with their lives.

CHAPTER 11

*D*aidan looked around, checking to make sure the discreet security was in place. No one would be able to land on the island unannounced, no one would be able to attack Taina, his home, or his company. He'd made sure of that. He exchanged a few words with his chief of security and then switched off the phone and turned to Taina. He forgot his worries instantly. She'd never looked more beautiful. The burnt orange satin of her evening dress made her look like the setting sun, vibrant and eclipsing all else with her beauty. She turned to him with eyes bright with excitement. She looked like a flower in full sun—giving forth a beauty and inner radiance that he'd never before seen in her.

It made him swear again never to allow anyone to hurt her. She wouldn't have liked the security measures if she knew how extensive they were, but he wasn't going to take any chances.

"Daidan! Look over there. Don't the barges look glorious?"

He followed her gaze out to the gulf which was as calm

and blue as a millpond in midsummer. He could almost have believed he was back at home in Ma'in, for the brilliance of the color—except the heat wasn't as fierce. He'd return there again, soon, with Taina. Turned out he had nothing to prove after all. All he needed was Taina.

"It was inspired. But aren't you always?"

"Not always," she said wryly. "But I probably will be in the future. I'm somehow feeling that my inspiration is going to continue for some time to come."

"Because you're happy."

She nodded. "I am." She glanced once more at the colorful barges, which edged ever closer to the island. "Or I will be when this afternoon's over." Their visitors were leaning on the boats' railings, their beautiful clothes lifting in the warm breeze, fingers outstretched as people pointed to the castle which stood behind them. Despite the fact that most of it was in ruins, it was still stunning. On three sides its stone walls soared up from the blue waters of the lake. It was on the fourth side that she and Daidan stood waiting for their guests to arrive. The collapse of the outer wall had proved a bonus in modern times, as events could be staged in the amphitheater of the castle ruins.

They walked down to the wharf by the castle and waited for their guests to disembark. Their staff lined up ready to hand out presents and information about the afternoon's entertainment while Daidan and Taina prepared to greet them.

Daidan squeezed her hand. "Feeling okay?"

She smiled. "The best. The morning sickness seems to have disappeared—thank goodness—and our people have been brilliant. They've covered all eventualities."

Daidan's mouth tightened, unable to rid himself of the nagging doubt that there might be something, some detail, he'd missed. "I certainly hope so."

She frowned. "You're not worried about anything?"

He didn't answer. Instead he held up his hand in greeting as the two boats came in on either side of the jetty. Taina scanned the boats, Daidan's reaction suddenly having made her nervous. But there was no one there who shouldn't be. No one who could threaten her happiness.

Daidan and Taina separated as they greeted their guests. Their staff mingled, handing out the programs and champagne to the guests as they drifted into the auditorium and took their seats, their necks craning as they admired the stunning backdrop to the performance—the gray stone of the medieval walls that soared into the blue of a perfect summer sky.

After a brief greeting from Daidan, the orchestra began and music filled the castle keep. Slowly the curtain rose on the stage and twelve models emerged, dressed in clinging white evening gowns, sky-high heels and dripping with diamonds from their new Northern Lights collection. The combined beauty and brilliance of the models and the jewelry in the bright sunshine was met by an audible gasp. It was almost blinding and that was exactly the impact Daidan and Taina had wanted. Daidan had only invited a few journalists he knew well. He'd arranged for his own photographers and TV cameras to support them. He had to be in control of it all. *Nothing* had been left to chance.

Lights flashed as the models posed and descended from the stage to walk amongst the guests before returning backstage under the watchful eye of security. The first set of models were wearing the designs the design team had put together. As each model emerged, posed for best effect, and then swept down and mingled with the guests, the style and branding became more and more obvious, more distilled. And then the final group of models emerged and the guests went wild. Taina's designs were amongst them—edgy and sophisticated. The collection not only showcased the quality of diamonds which were being mined by the company, but also the distinctive Scandinavian design ethos—spare and stunning. They needed nothing more to add to their brilliance.

Taina watched with satisfaction and relief as even the most hardened of the jewelry mavens became excited, talking to the designers and looking over her way as the designers referenced her work.

DAIDAN RE-CHECKED the position of the security guards, dressed in dinner suits, who were positioned at strategic points. There were enough diamonds here to ensure the wellbeing of a small country for a year. And each guard had been designated specific models to watch over. Their build and authority were as much a part of the display as the models and the setting.

He dipped his head to Taina as a model wearing the centerpiece to the collection walked past.

"You were correct, darling. That piece—it needed the flaw to make it more beautiful, more unique."

"Ha! I knew you'd agree eventually." She smoothed her hand down his immaculate black dinner jacket and he took hold of it and gripped it tightly. "I have excellent taste, you have to admit."

"True," he grinned. "You chose me."

"Did I? I rather thought it was the other way around."

Although they were all still seated, waiting for the concert to begin, he kept tight hold of her hand. He wanted to know where she was at every moment of today's events. Word had it that something was going to be attempted and he was damned sure that no one and nothing would get to Taina. Mind you, she'd be hard to miss. He glanced admiringly at her in the orange satin strapless evening dress. Her skin was tanned, making her violet eyes more intense and her blond hair even brighter. She stood out against the men in their black tuxes and the models in their all white dresses, as if all the others were only there to showcase her beauty.

But she wasn't perfect. Daidan knew that now. Just as he wasn't. Although he'd always known *that*. But her vulnerabilities and complexities made her even more precious. Their world wasn't black and white as he'd always treated it, but held the complexities and beauty of a rainbow, just as light split from the diamonds showered color over the gray stone walls of the castle.

Suddenly the spotlights moved and the color and intensity changed as they focused on the orchestra. The horn section began to play and the audience went silent, impressed by the opening bars which blended the majestic— with the horns and drums—with the lyrical melody of the flutes and violins. It was patriotic music—music which described throwing off the shackles of slavery and becoming free. Daidan glanced at Taina who sat, like all the others, entranced by the power of the music. He knew why she'd chosen Sibelius's *Finlandia*. It had been her idea to hold a short concert of Finnish music to further brand the event. But it went deeper than that.

He watched as she spread her fingers over her stomach, her thumb stroking over its gentle swell and he placed his hand over hers. Their gaze met briefly before she looked back at the stage and he continued to look around, searching out shadowy areas, nodding to people he knew to be watching, but whom no one else was aware of. He felt uneasy. No doubt simply because of the amount of jewelry that was all together in one place. That would be enough to make anyone concerned. But it was more than that. He felt a shiver down his spine, as if something wasn't right. He continued to scan

the castle and beyond. There was nothing out of place. Then
he heard the sound of a motorboat approaching. Late guests,
no doubt. He watched a couple alight on the jetty and
narrowed his eyes. He was a little surprised to see them—
they'd declined their invitation because of pressure of business. And yet here they were. It was Mark, a fellow diamond
mine owner from Australia and his girlfriend—*not* his wife.
He disapproved of his brazen attitude but remembered a few
comments the Australian's wife—Amelia—had made about
him last year and realized that she was under no illusions
about her husband. They were being stopped by security.
He'd better go and greet them. He was about to tell Taina
that some late guests had arrived before he stopped himself.
She was utterly lost in the music and he hadn't the heart to
disturb her. Instead he kissed her hand and quietly slipped
away.

ONCE THE MUSIC FINISHED, Taina turned around. She'd
vaguely heard a boat approach. No doubt people who'd
missed the barge. She glanced around to see who it was but
someone spoke to her and she had to turn away. By the time
she looked up, whoever had arrived late had been seated.

Despite her reassurances to Daidan about lack of
morning sickness, she still felt a little queasy and she sat back
and closed her eyes and listened to the music swell and fill
the small space with its vibrations. When the music stopped
and the applause began she opened her eyes to find Daidan
had returned. He wiped away a stray tear from her cheek.

"Are you sure you're okay?"

She wiped her forehead which was feeling clammy. The
blue sky was beginning to mist over, holding in the heat of
the late afternoon. "Probably just the humidity. I think I'll
just slip away and get some sea air for a few moments."

"I'll come with you."

"No, I'll be fine. You stay and look after our guests. We can't both leave."

She rose and, waving in greeting to different guests, she left the auditorium to the strains of Sibelius's *The Swan of Tuonela*.

She knew the castle inside out. It had been her playground as a kid. She made her way up the inner wall and looked out from a higher level, down to the assembled crowd, all eyes on the performer, Karita, who had begun to sing one of Sibelius's songs—*The Diamond on the March Snow*.

While Karita's beautiful soprano voice filled the castle, Taina inhaled the fresh sea air that blew in from the gulf, and looked down on the brilliant spectacle. Some of the spotlights were trained on Karita, while others lit the castle walls, and yet others subtly lit the audience, making their jewelry glitter.

Taina leaned back against the rough stone wall and felt a glow of pride. The jewelry had looked amazing—they'd be new classics—and the launch was going without a hitch. She felt better already and descended the steps. She was about to return to her seat when she took a last look around and saw a woman surreptitiously showing her neighbor the necklace she wore beneath a silk scarf. It caught one of the spotlights and Taina recognized it instantly. She narrowed her eyes. She knew the diamonds that glittered around the woman's throat well—but she didn't know the woman. The diamonds were her own—the Kielo necklace that she'd given away. But not to this woman.

The woman glanced at the man beside her and quickly re-covered the necklace with her scarf. Taina's heart thudded sickeningly as her gaze switched to the man who had his back to her as he turned to speak to the person behind him. She swallowed. The thick, sun-burned neck, the closely-cropped blond hair. It couldn't be. He hadn't been on the guest list. She'd checked over and over. Daidan had said that Mark couldn't make it. Then he turned and looked straight at her, a slow smile spreading over his full lips. She felt the cold chill of horror seep through her body. She stumbled away from the auditorium and fell back against the cold stone wall, its flints digging into the bare flesh of her shoulders. All her instinct told her to run but instead she staggered out of sight of her guests and tried to recover herself. She swiped the tears away from her eyes and gripped the stone walls with determination. She wouldn't run this time.

Slowly and deliberately she made her way to the end of the row where Mark and his girlfriend had been seated. She joined in the applause at the end of the song and waited for people to rise. A brief interval had been planned to accommodate people's drinking and gossiping requirements, as well as to have their models move around, continually showcasing their collection. And their guests loved it. Cameras flashed, spontaneous applause broke out as new pieces were spotted. By the time Taina was able to move toward the late arriving couple, Mark had disappeared, but his girlfriend was there, looking lost, the silk scarf securely wrapped around her neck once more, covering the priceless necklace. Taina's necklace.

"Hello," Taina said, holding out a hand. "I don't believe we've met?"

The girl smiled, a bright trusting smile and Taina instantly knew she hadn't the first idea what she was wearing around her beautiful neck. "I'm Natalya," the girl said with a heavy Russian accent. "I'm here with Mark."

"Ah, that would explain it."

Natalya frowned. "What?"

"Why you're wearing that necklace. May I see?"

Natalya looked around and smiled nervously. "Mark didn't want me to show anyone just yet."

"Then come with me and show me somewhere more private." Taina smiled encouragingly at the young girl. She couldn't hate her. She was simply a beautiful young woman who'd been sucked into a world beyond her experience. Mark was her lifeline, her passport for a future out of Russia. "Come."

Taina led the girl behind the castle walls. "May I see?"

Natalya nodded uncertainly and loosened her scarf and revealed the necklace.

Taina bit her lip. It was hers all right. "It's a shame to hide its beauty under a scarf."

"It's only for a while. Mark said I should take the scarf off when we were on the boat, leaving the island."

"Ah." Taina nodded. She suddenly saw exactly what Mark was up to. Mark must know that Taina hadn't told Daidan she'd been raped. Mark had told her exactly what would happen if she did. And she'd accepted the threats, backed up as they were by her own fears over Daidan's reaction. But he did want Daidan to believe she'd had a relationship with Mark, and that she'd given him the necklace. That's the only reason she could think of why Natalya had been told to reveal it only when they were safely back on the boat. A last-minute revelation to hit Daidan where it hurt. "Thank you for showing me. You'd better cover it up now." She watched Natalya cover up the necklace as a plan formed in her mind. She glanced at Daidan who was busy talking to a group of American diamond merchants. "I wonder if you'd do me a favor?"

Natalya smiled. "Of course."

"During the next interlude would you mind letting my husband know that I'm feeling a little faint and had to return to the house? I'll be back in around half an hour."

"Sure. No problem."

"Good. And don't forget to keep your necklace covered. I think it best that you do as Mark suggests."

Taina watched Natalya return to her seat. As Taina suspected, Mark wasn't there. She looked around and saw him standing in an arch of the castle, waiting for her. She wouldn't run this time, she repeated. It was time to rid herself of the fear that had been haunting her once and for all. She glanced at the time and then walked over to Mark. The presentation would be beginning shortly—a video followed by Daidan and her on center stage. She had to get this over with as quickly as possible.

She walked past Mark and he followed her up some stone steps to a private upper walkway, close to the projectionist and light operator, but private nonetheless. She knew he was up to something—something which would no doubt to deprive Daidan and her of the victory they wanted from the launch. And she had to find out what. But just being in his company made her feel sick. Each time she looked at him, the memories flooded back—of the last time she'd seen him, in a rambling villa on the island of Antigua, where there'd been no escape from him. He'd taken what he'd wanted from her and had shown no mercy. But she was going to stand her ground this time. She couldn't risk Daidan confronting Mark.

At the top of a flight of stairs she turned to look at him stealthily approaching her, just as he had when he'd come to her in Antigua. He thrust his hands in his pockets and sauntered up to her, grinning from ear to ear.

"Darling," he said as he kissed her on both cheeks. His grin turned to a leer, as his hand lingered on her waist and gave her a surreptitious pinch. "It's been too long."

Taina forced herself not to slap him away. She could do it,

she thought. She could do it for Daidan. "What a surprise. I didn't see your name on the guest list."

He raised an eyebrow. "Surely you didn't expect me *not* to come?"

"You didn't reply to the invitation. I thought…"

He stepped closer. "What did you think?"

She shrugged. "I thought you must have more pressing business."

"And what could be more pressing than seeing my favorite girl? Besides—" He winked. "I *wanted* to surprise you. Believe me, it was always my intention to come."

"Really? And yet your wife didn't seem to be aware of that."

His expression darkened slightly but his smile remained fixed. "My wife is more interested in your husband than my whereabouts, believe me. Didn't you know?"

"I don't know what you're talking about."

"They had an affair before he came to Finland. An affair which I'm sure has continued. She's besotted with him."

Taina didn't believe a word of it. She knew Daidan and she knew he'd spoken the truth when he'd stated his loyalty to her. But she could see that Mark believed it. "You're jealous. That's what this is all about. You wanted to get back at him. That's why you want Natalya to show off the necklace as you leave. You'll be out of his reach, but he'll know you took it from me. He'll know that—" She couldn't bring herself to finish the sentence.

"That I *had* you, fully and completely. Yes, you're right, I do want him to know. Why else would you have given me the necklace, unless you were infatuated with me?"

"Because you made me," she ground out, remembering the threats he'd made, the lies he'd said he'd tell unless she gave him the Kielo necklace.

"I simply showed you how it would look to everyone else.

Poor little rich girl Taina had always wanted me and left her husband to find me. Threw herself at me, tried to buy my affections with a priceless necklace. Tried to make me leave my wife for her. But she failed because I didn't want her, and she returned to her husband."

She shook her head. "No one would believe that."

"And why not? Sounds convincing to me. Especially when I mention the drugs. You looked so fetching in the video I made—so docile and compliant. So… willing." He grinned. "And then you disappeared for the rest of the year, God knows where. Maybe a long visit to a rehabilitation center? Yeah, I reckon people would believe that all right. Especially given your mother's history."

She shook her head. "It wasn't like that. You'd put those drugs in my drink. I couldn't move."

"Prove it."

"You know I can't."

She drew in a deep breath, trying to control her instinctive desire to get the hell away from this man. But she couldn't leave. She'd told Daidan she'd never run again and she wouldn't. This time she'd stay and sort it out. "I was stupid then. Stupid enough to believe you'd follow through. Stupid enough to believe Daidan and I couldn't withstand your lies. I was stupid, naïve and scared. But I'm not now. Tell me why you're here. Surely it can't be only jealousy."

"You *are* getting less naïve. You're right. I've moved beyond that. I'm playing with the big boys now."

"What are you talking about?"

"You think I'm only here to get at the media darlings, Daidan and Taina? Well, I'm not. That's merely to rub salt into the wound which I'm about to inflict."

She jerked her head up suddenly. "What wound?"

Mark's sly smile make her shiver. "You'll see."

"What? Tell me!"

Mark glanced at his watch, nodded smugly and pointed. "Just watch the stage."

She looked over to where Mark had indicated. "I don't see anything."

"You wouldn't. That's the point. My partners and I don't want anyone to see, until it's too late."

She swung back to face him. "Too late for what?"

"For you... for Daidan... for your company." He reached over and pulled her toward him.

She yanked herself out of his grip and stepped away. "I'm warning you. Leave now and you might be able to leave in one piece."

He laughed. "You? Threaten me? That's rich. I seem to remember you were easily overpowered."

"Drugs do that to people," she spat out.

He gripped the string of diamonds around her neck and grabbed her with his other hand and pulled her hard against his body. This time she couldn't move away. "Let go!" She struggled, helpless in his cast-iron grip.

"No." There was no humor now in his face, only a steely determination. "No, Taina. It doesn't work like that. It's no longer only about me. I'm working for people more powerful than you and your precious husband can imagine."

A wave of icy dread seized her. "Who?"

His lips curled into a mirthless smile. "You really want to know?"

She nodded. "Tell me. This needs to finish. Now!"

She tried to knee him where it hurt but he deflected her attempt. "God, you turn me on when you're like this." Before she could react his hand was around her neck, gripping it as he pulled her face to his and kissed her.

DAIDAN LOOKED across to where he'd last seen Taina, talking

to Mark's girlfriend in the shadows of the castle walls. The girl had returned to her seat but Taina hadn't. She'd been gone for ten minutes and he was beginning to worry. As the last note of the soprano settled into the air, there was a brief lull of silence before enthusiastic applause burst forth. He rose, clapping along with the others as they began stretching their legs, walking around the courtyard, topping up their drinks, eating and admiring the ancient castle. After leaving one particularly persistent group of people, Daidan began to walk over to where he'd last seen Taina when a piece of jewelry caught his eye, revealed by a loose scarf as it flew away in the stiffening breeze. He stared, not believing what he was seeing. The Kielo necklace? Taina's necklace? Here?

He felt as if he'd been struck. All he could see was the beauty of the necklace, its cold glittering diamonds sparkling in the stray beam of sunlight, taunting him with chilling clarity. Even before he could think it through, he knew. A cold blind fury overtook him as he glanced over at the empty seat beside the woman who was quickly replacing the scarf around her neck, hiding the necklace once more.

"Natalya, is it?"

"Yes." The woman smiled nervously and extended her hand. "I met your wife earlier. She asked me to let you know she didn't feel well and had returned to the house for a while."

"Ah, right." What was Taina up to? Before he found out he first wanted to reclaim what was hers. He looked at Natalya's throat where the jewels were now hidden by the scarf that was now back in place. "Your necklace. May I see it?"

She tilted her head coquettishly to one side. "Sure." She flicked her blond hair to one side and pulled away her scarf revealing a deep cleavage, which she seemed keener to display, and the necklace.

"It's beautiful." He narrowed his gaze. "Who made it?"

She shrugged and pouted her pretty lips. "I don't know. I think Mark did tell me. Apparently it's priceless. I'm not meant to show it to anyone until I'm back on the boat but your wife spotted it, too." She shrugged. "I couldn't resist showing it off. It'll be back in the vault tomorrow."

"Of course. Such things are much safer in a vault, where no one can see them, or claim them." He paused. "May I see the clasp?"

"Sure." She turned around and held up her hair.

In one swift movement, Daidan had undone the necklace.

She gasped and turned around as Daidan held it up to the light. "As I thought. It's Finnish. Would you mind? My wife would be fascinated. It's a family piece, you see."

The woman's face had gone white. "But… Mark wouldn't like—"

"Don't worry. I'll clear it with Mark. Where is he?"

She shrugged nervously, fingering her now bare throat. "I haven't seen him. He disappeared about ten minutes ago."

Daidan immediately slipped the diamonds into his pocket and walked over to where he'd last seen Taina. Behind the castle walls were a maze of half-ruined rooms which were out of bounds to the public. He knew instinctively it would be there that he'd find them. Just as he knew that she was still trying to protect him from the knowledge that Mark had raped her. She was trying to deal with the situation alone. But there was no way he was going to let her.

He cursed softly as he ran up the stone steps to the upper floors. He'd imposed so many security measures, done so much to prevent such a thing as this happening, and yet it *had* happened. The most priceless jewel of all, Taina, had been caught in the security measures he'd imposed. He'd trapped her in a net of his own making, with the man he most wanted to protect her from.

When he reached the top of the stairs he stopped in a

cloud of dust. Taina was in Mark's arms and they were kissing.

Fury roared through Daidan and he bridged the gap between him and the kissing couple in a split second, hauling Mark from Taina. A misplaced punch from Mark sent Taina flying down into the dirt. Daidan gripped Mark's shirt at his throat and slammed him against the wall.

"Daidan! No!" Taina scrambled to her feet and tried to pull him off Mark. "No, don't."

Daidan brought back his arm to land a punch on Mark but through the bloody haze he felt Taina's soft touch on his arm and slowly her pleas filtered through to him. He turned in confusion. Why the hell didn't she want him to sort this animal out after what he'd done?

"Don't," she appealed again.

He pushed Mark up against the wall and let him fall to his feet. "Christ, Daidan," gasped Mark as he doubled up, coughing. "Thought you'd lost your mind for a moment there."

"No, I've lost it now, letting you go." Daidan stepped back as an added security against him hitting Mark again.

"She begged me for it, so what could I do?" Mark dusted off his jacket. "A nice piece. I can see why you took her back. We were just having a bit of fun. You know?"

"No, I don't know." Daidan didn't turn around to Taina. He wasn't going to take his eyes off that snake. "It didn't look like fun to me. Taina?" There was silence. He turned around then. "Taina?" But she was gone.

A cold fear gripped his heart that had nothing to do with the man in front of him and all to do with the woman he'd believed had loved him but who hadn't stuck around to tell him so. Had everything that had gone on between them these past months been a charade, a parade of lies? Simply a trick to get what she wanted after all?

"Run away, has she?" Mark taunted. "Didn't like being caught out by her husband. Sorry, mate."

Anger and frustration beat back the fear as Daidan focused on Mark. He'd deal with Taina later. But now he'd deal with Mark.

CHAPTER 12

A sudden sound made Daidan twist back around, ready to pounce, all thought of calm gone. Mark was trying to walk away.

Daidan stepped wide, blocking his path.

If Taina had looked fearful, that was nothing to how the Aussie looked. His eyes shifted around, searching for escape like a trapped animal. Which he was, thought Daidan.

"Where do you think you're going, Mark?"

Mark half-laughed and shifted uneasily from foot to foot. "Back to the concert, of course. The second act should be starting soon. Believe me, I don't want to miss that."

He'd made a promise to Taina to control his temper. No more fights. No more violent outbursts. But his blood pounded with an anger so fierce he could hardly think at all. He advanced on his prey, just as he was sure Mark had done to the woman Daidan loved more than life itself. He wouldn't let the old primitive instinct take over. He *wouldn't*. He'd give Mark one last chance to make amends.

"Okay, have it your way. You can leave now, if you like. Take your girlfriend and get the hell out of here."

"You're making a mistake. I've done nothing wrong. Twelve months ago I simply saw a chance with Taina and took it." Mark tried to side-step Daidan but Daidan wasn't inclined to move an inch. Mark shrugged and grimaced. "You know what women are like."

"You tell me."

Mark was so egotistical, he'd obviously lost the ability to pick up danger signals. And Daidan was sure he'd been giving off enough of them.

"What can I say? I have women throwing themselves at me all the time. She came on to me. Reckon she'd been drinking a bit, taking a few drugs, and was having a bit of fun, a bit of laugh with everyone. You know how it is…"

"Do I?"

"Yeah, sure you do." He shrugged. "You know how women get, touchy feely, putting their hands on your arm and all that. You know if they're up for it."

"Because she touches you on the arm, you think she wants sex?"

"Hey, it was more than that."

"Tell me what happened next."

"You really want to know?"

"Yes, I really do."

He shrugged. "Not much to say. And, look, I'm sorry you had to find out this way, but I did what any man would have done in the same situation. What you've been doing with my wife for years."

Daidan frowned. "Amelia?"

"Yeah, I know you loved her."

"That was over years ago. Before I even came to Finland. Before you'd even met her. But no doubt you told Taina."

"I may have done. Can't remember."

"Tell me what you can remember, then."

"Hey, you don't want to go there. Come on, let's get back to the girls."

"I want to know what happened."

"Why would you care? Everyone knows your marriage is a sham, just a commercial arrangement jacked up with Taina's father."

Daidan took a step forward and Mark took one back, slamming himself against the stone wall of the castle keep. "Tell me what happened," Daidan repeated.

"We had sex, what do you think happened?"

"What do I think happened? I *know* what happened. I just wanted to hear you admit it. You raped her, you bastard and you're going to pay."

"Rape? No way. And you dare lay a hand on me and you'll be finished." He barked a cruel laugh. "What am I saying? In a few minutes you'll be finished anyway."

Daidan tried to count to ten, tried to control the rage that burned in his gut. Mark must have taken his silence for agreement. And that's when he made his final mistake.

"She's a tart, just like all the others. She's not worth us falling out over. A rough diamond that stayed rough. Just like her mother before her, from what I hear."

Mark could insult Daidan, he could reduce his business to rubble, but there was no way he could insult Taina.

"Didn't anyone tell you that diamonds are made beautiful under pressure?" Daidan moved away and saw Mark relax, just as Daidan swung his fist into Mark's face. Mark hit the floor with a dull thud and Daidan walked out, down the narrow staircase and out into the auditorium.

At that moment the music began—the music they'd selected to open the short promotional video clip. Daidan glanced at the screen and then froze. The image was different.

TAINA RACED along the stone corridors of the castle, trying to get to the projection room as quickly as possible. That comment Mark had made, it had to do with the presentation. He must have tampered with it. And with the Russians behind him, God knows what he'd done. Was it the video he'd claimed he'd made of him raping her while she was drowsy with drugs? Footage which would scandalize and damn them. Or was it cobbled together lies about their mines? It wouldn't matter if the footage was of their own mines, or the Russians, the seeds of doubt and controversy would be sewn in the minds of their influential audience and the future Daidan had worked so hard for would be ruined.

She ran panting into the makeshift projection room. "Stop the film," she shouted at the surprised operator. The man looked up at his boss who nodded.

"But we've already begun it. We're under strict instructions from the Prince to—"

"I don't care what's been said." She glanced at the images that were beginning to appear on the screen—images that she'd never seen before, of a mine that wasn't theirs. "It needs to stop." She rushed up to the computer screen and was about to press a button—any button, when the supervisor spoke to the operator. "Go ahead, do as Madame Mustonen requires."

With a few swift keystrokes the strange images morphed into a blank screen showing simply the company's logo and the same music.

"It's the wrong film. The wrong film! Find the original one, the one that my husband gave you yesterday. Find it!"

She looked over the supervisor's shoulder, at the different versions of the video. Mark had even named his video the same as theirs. "Check the date."

She scanned down the details of the files. "There, that one." It was dated yesterday, at the time she'd made the final changes to it. "Run that one immediately. But filter it in slowly, like this was meant to happen."

The supervisor took over and created a swirling effect from which emerged the logo once more. He changed the music so it rose to a crescendo and then began the video. Taina went over to the ruins of the window which overlooked the stage and watched the film being projected onto the vast screen above the stage, and held her breath. The mists cleared from over a watery, wooded Finland and formed their logo. So far so good. And then the landscape changed into the glamorous and lush fabrics upon which diamonds spilled and then the images panned out to a vibrant, bustling New York. It was the right video. Everything was on track. She returned to the supervisor and looked around.

"Where's that operator gone?"

The supervisor looked up and Taina could tell from his expression that he was innocent of what had happened. He looked around. "He shouldn't have gone anywhere."

"Who was he? I hadn't seen him before."

"He's new. My usual operator was sick."

She nodded. It all fitted. "Give me the memory stick with the wrong presentation on and delete it from the computer. I don't want any more mistakes."

"I'm sorry. I don't know how it happened. There won't be any more mistakes."

She'd make sure there wouldn't be. She took his phone and rang security and soon a couple of burly men had been briefed and were in place. She glanced at the presentation which would be over in a few minutes. She and Daidan had to get back for their big moment when they took the stage and the evening concluded.

SHE SWEPT up her gown in her hands and ran through the ruins back to where she'd left Daidan and Mark. There was no one there. Just a trail of blood that went down the stairs. Christ! Was it Daidan's or Mark's?

But there was no time to think about it. She had to get down to the stage before the music ended. She ran through the back corridors, empty except for the occasional security guard who looked at her with distant professionalism and nodded respectfully as she flew past. Suddenly she slammed into Daidan.

"Daidan! Are you okay? Did he hurt you?"

"What happened to the video? Where have you been?"

"There was a problem—" The music played and she took his hand which was gripped into a fist and pulled him onto the stage. She smiled and he formed some semblance of a smile. She lifted their joined fists as they'd agreed but saw blood on his. She felt her smile waiver and she pulled it back to their sides once more.

She was furious that Mark had not only tried to ruin her marriage but also that he'd nearly managed to ruin the culmination of her and Daidan's hard work. She knew how much it all meant to Daidan. Then she took Daidan's fist again, blood stained and all, and held it aloft in the air. Let everyone, including Mark, wherever he was, see that she and Daidan were strong and wouldn't be defeated.

Suddenly Daidan pulled away and she felt her heart freeze by the doubt in his eyes when he looked at her. He backed away a couple of paces and took his place before the microphone, framed by the logo and the image of a simple trailing diamond necklace she'd designed. He took one last look at her and then turned to their guests, spread out before them, shaded by the low evening sunshine by the castle walls. The spotlights which ranged along the castle walls were focused on the stage. And Taina stepped back so she could see better. Daidan filled the stage with his presence. His dark beauty was stunning against the bright lights and glittering diamonds. His eyes flashed with confidence and authority and his deep voice filled the auditorium. She couldn't take in his words, but she knew what he'd planned to say so it didn't matter. Then suddenly, too soon, he stepped aside and looked at her. He didn't look at her with invitation, but a wariness which broke her heart. But it wasn't time for her to fall apart. It was time for her to be strong.

She walked into the bright spotlight, cameras flashing as she looked out at the crowd which shimmered under the light of its own jewelry. It was a spotlight she'd been at pains to avoid all her life. But she was ready for it now.

She began the prepared speech, thanking everyone for coming, referring back to her family history—the good bits anyway—and to the land of her birth from which the diamonds were being mined. Then she halted, caught by the shimmering light, arrested by what really filled her heart. She turned to Daidan and reached back and held out her hand to him, imploring him with her eyes to come to her. She didn't need him to make her feel strong because she felt strong already. She reached back because she wanted him—not needed him—to share the moment with her.

"And I'd like to thank my husband for having faith in me, and, I hope, trusting in that faith now, more than ever." She kissed his bloodied hand. "The future," she said into the microphone. She stepped toward him. "*Our* future," she said to him alone. He nodded slowly. "Our future?" he repeated tentatively. Then he pulled her to him within full view of everyone and kissed her tenderly on the lips. When he moved away he sighed. "Our future," he said again, this time with a certainty that was missing before. Suddenly she was aware of the uproar of clapping and whistling from the audience. Their distinguished guests were showing very undistinguished approval of their kiss. She turned to the audience and laughed, suddenly remembering her last duty on stage—to announce the second performance by the soprano. She leaned toward the microphone while Daidan kept her hand firmly within his. "Ladies and gentleman, Karita!"

On the wings of the rising applause Daidan and Taina left the stage. She looked at his hand, covered in blood and beginning to swell. "Come with me. Now!" He looked like he couldn't believe she was ordering him around. "*Now*, Daidan. We're going to get this business cleaned up once and for all."

He raised his bloodied hand. "This, you mean?"

"Everything. There's never going to be any bad blood between us from now on."

Without stopping to hear his answer Taina took his bloodied hand and led him to the caterer's vans which were hidden around the rear of the castle. She walked into one of them to be met by three shocked and bewildered expressions. She ignored them and spotted the sinks. "This will do." She looked at the staff. "If you wouldn't mind?" The expressions continued to be bewildered. "Please leave us."

The bewilderment turned to relief as the washing-up staff shot out of the caravan. Taina turned on the running water and took Daidan's hand in her own. He winced as the water hit it. She washed it in silence as words tumbled in her mind in confusion. In the end the silence continued as she dried it. "No cuts, just badly bruised." She eyed him fiercely. "I guess you hurt him."

He shook his head. "I can't get the two of you going off together out of my head. You and him. Alone."

She dried her hands on a tea towel and put her hands on her hips. "Mark and I together. Yeah. And that's what I wanted. Any idea why?"

"Because you wanted to be alone with him?"

"Exactly. Because I knew he was up to something. He

wasn't here only to taunt me, only to make you crazy. There was something else and I had to get to the bottom of it. And I did. He'd switched sides, Daidan. He was in bed with the Russians."

Daidan's eyes widened. "The Russians? What? How did you figure that out?"

"It was something he said. I knew there had to be more than his jealousy. And he couldn't wait to boast about it. 'Playing with the big boys' is how he described it."

"Is that why you ran off as soon as I'd arrived? I thought you were afraid of me. I thought…"

"What?"

"That I'd interrupted something you didn't want me to know about."

"You thought wrong," she said severely. "How can you have so little faith in me?"

"It's not faith in you that's missing. It's faith in myself to keep you."

She sighed. "Oh, Daidan! The only reason I left was because the video had just begun and it was wrong. Mark had swapped presentations. Between them they'd put together clips of the failing, slipshod Russian mine, not ours. And, apparently clips of me… and Mark. You see he drugged me. It made me look… willing."

"And he was going to show that?"

"Yes. But I got to the control room in time. Mark had planted an operator there. He left as soon as I arrived. We managed to fudge the beginning and replace it with our presentation."

"It could have been the end. Not only of your reputation, but mine, the company's, our whole future."

"Forget it." She clutched his arms tightly. She could see the fury about what might have happened flame in his eyes.

"Forget it, Daidan. Forget him. It's over. But we have to get back. We have to finish this event off."

Daidan nodded and opened the door for her. "Let's go."

Hand in hand they ran down to the side stage. There they stopped. They turned to each other. "Do I look okay?" she asked.

"You look stronger and more beautiful than I've ever seen you before."

He took her face in his hands and kissed her, just as the music ended. They pulled apart. "Ready, Madame Mustonen?"

She smiled. "More than ready, my Prince."

"Just one more thing." He took the diamonds from his pocket. "Turn around." She did as he told her and he lifted her hair and fastened the original kielo necklace around her neck while removing her own. Then he took her hand and together they walked onto the stage to great applause. The low sun illuminated them, shining off her silk dress, making her diamond necklace sparkle.

IT WAS LATE before Taina waved the last of their visitors off on the boat back to Helsinki and to their luxury hotels. She and Daidan would be joining them later for supper. In the meantime, they had a few hours by themselves. She turned away from the calm waters of the gulf and looked to Daidan. He stood watching her, hands on his hips, a smile on his lips.

"That's the last of them."

"And thank God for that. It went well though, didn't it?"

"Thanks to you. We'd be in a very different position now if you hadn't worked out what Mark was up to."

"And not just Mark. He was just the puppet. I'm still worried about the Russians."

"No need," said Daidan pulling her into his embrace as they walked back to the house.

Taina stopped abruptly and stared at him. "What do you mean, no need? They almost destroyed our new business!"

"I spoke with Nikolai—Vadim's father."

"Vadim? Who took Rory's estate from her?"

"That's the one. Well, it seems Mark had suggested this little ploy to them and they'd gone along with it. No risk to them. But we've come to an arrangement. Or a truce. They have their market, we have ours and we've agreed not to encroach on each other's territories."

"For now."

"For now is good enough for me." They stopped at the long veranda that fronted the house, floating above the water.

"There's nothing better." She stood on tiptoe and kissed him.

He grinned. "Just as well we have a few hours before we go to the city to join the others."

"Just as well."

She squeezed his hand and she caught a slight wince in the corner of his eye. She held up his hand and inspected it. "That was some punch you gave him, wasn't it?"

He narrowed his eyes. "Maybe."

"I'm glad you hit him."

"What?"

"I'm glad. He had it coming to him." She paused. "What are we going to do about him? No doubt he'll still have copies of the video."

"I'll contact Amelia and tell her everything. She'll get someone to check his files and clear them out. She doesn't want anything to do with him anymore. She's told me that she's finished with him. Between the two of us, he's ruined. He's no longer of any use to the Russians. They know that a deal with us will be more beneficial than working with someone like Mark, who didn't do what he'd said he'd do."

She shook her head and sighed. "It's the end, isn't it? The end of all of this."

"Nearly."

"Nearly? You don't still believe I returned to Finland to use you?"

"As it happens, I do, because it's true. You wanted the company, you wanted the child."

"No." She shook her head, frowning, wondering how he could believe that, after everything that had happened. "It's not like that."

"It think it is, but it's okay."

"Okay? So... you believe I set out to use you and yet you're still talking to me?"

"I'm here because it wasn't only the company and the child. You wanted something else from me, something I hadn't given you enough of in the brief time we were together. Something I'm determined to give you every day of our lives together."

She smiled and raised an eyebrow. "And that is?"

"You know..." He tugged her to him and kissed her. "You know."

"Maybe," she said when she emerged from another kiss. "But I'd like to hear you say it."

"I never *told* you I loved you, although I did. I never *showed* you that I loved you, although I felt it. And I'm never going to *stop* showing you how much I love you for the rest of my life."

She wrapped her arms around him and rested her cheek against his chest. "I like the sound of that."

EPILOGUE

The night breeze was warm against Taina's face as she sat on deck, watching the island grow ever larger. She could just make out a dark silhouette at the window. He was in the lounge, with the fire's flames flickering behind him. Just as he had been that first night, eighteen months before. It seemed a lifetime away.

Suddenly bright green lights, shot with palest pink, floated up into the sky and she gasped in delight. She never tired of the northern lights—aurora borealis—but tonight, as they unfurled like celestial flowers against the star-studded sky, they seemed extra special as she held her sleepy little girl close, and her new secret even closer. She shivered. But not from cold, from anticipation.

"Papa!" Mirette stuck out her arms as Daidan opened the door and he picked her up with swoop and gave her a big hug before turning to Taina.

"Mustn't forget your Mama," he said, brushing his lips against hers.

"I'll make sure you don't," said Taina.

"Sounds interesting," replied Daidan as he took Mirette down the corridor to her room.

Taina went to the bedroom to shower while Daidan read Mirette her bedtime story. By the time she'd returned to the lounge, dressed only in a silk robe, Daidan was back in his position by the fire.

"That was quick," said Taina, turning the lock on the door behind her. "Is she asleep?"

"She was fast asleep before I got to the bottom of the page. Now, come here."

"Is that a command?"

"It certainly is."

"In that case, I'll think I'll stay here." She smiled as she perched on the edge of the couch, causing her robe to fall open and his gaze to drop to her bare thighs.

"So I can admire you better?"

"Of course. And while you're admiring me, you can tell me how the meeting with Anton Kuzmich went."

"Very satisfactory. They're being as cordial as they'll ever be and they're keeping to our agreement. And as formidable as Anton is, he's far more reasonable than his father. We've nothing to fear from them anymore."

"Good." It was as they'd anticipated. Their association with the Australian mines, now run single-handedly by Amelia, was going from strength to strength and it was a relief to know that there were no longer any threats—either personal or business—coming from the Kuzmich family.

"And you, Taina? You're later than I thought. How did your meeting go?"

"Very well. My new design has been made up. They used the diamonds we chose."

"What was the design again?"

"A pendant. A very sexy pendant designed to hang low. I have it on."

"Show me."

This time it was a command she wanted to obey. She walked over to him and slowly shrugged off her robe and let it fall to the floor. The heat of the open fire warmed her back and Daidan's gaze warmed her front which was dressed only in a diamond pendant that dangled between her breasts.

His throat convulsed as he reached out and traced the chain down to her breasts, before taking the diamond cluster in his fingers and turning it back and forth in the firelight, causing shards of light to flicker across the walls. Then his gaze caught hers and entranced, she watched as he licked the diamond before brushing first one nipple and then the other with it. She gasped and clenched her muscles inside as she tried to contain her arousal.

"It's beautiful, Taina. The setting you designed enhances its shape and color."

"I'm glad you like it. But that's not all I have to show you."

"Really?"

She took his hand and brought his palm to her mouth where she kissed it. Then she moved it down her neck, over her breasts and the diamond which lay between them, and down to her stomach where she stopped. He tried to move his hand down further to her sex, which was *so* ready for him, but she resisted.

"Taina?"

She moved his palm over her stomach in a brief caress, watching his reaction all the while. She could see the moment he understood. It was there, in the expression of his brown eyes, warm in the reflected firelight. He kissed her. "You're pregnant."

She nodded. "Confirmed by Dr Linna this afternoon. A little brother for Mirette to play with."

He kissed her again except this time his passion was unchecked as he trailed kisses down her neck to her breasts.

Then he lay her down before the fire and kissed her stomach, his hands caressing the place where a new life was forming. Then he moved down further and kissed her lower, where she ached for him. She closed her eyes and submitted to the bliss of his touch, a touch that promised a future full of the things she'd always wanted—love and a baby by her most beloved sheikh.

AFTERWORD

Thank you for reading *Wanted: A Baby by the Sheikh*. I hope you enjoyed it! Reviews are always welcome—they help me, and they help prospective readers to decide if they'd enjoy the book.

The other five books in the series are:

Wanted: A Wife for the Sheikh
The Sheikh's Bargain Bride
The Sheikh's Lost Lover
Awakened by the Sheikh
Claimed by the Sheikh

If you've read all of the above, why not try out one of my other books? There is the **Italian Romance** series which begins with *Perfect* (excerpt follows). Then there are two series set in New Zealand: **The Mackenzies**, and **New Zealand Brides**. Against a backdrop of beautiful New Zealand locations—deserted beaches, Wellington towers, snow-capped mountains—the Mackenzie and Connelly families fall in love. But expect some twists and turns!

You can check out all my books on the following pages. And, if you'd like to know when my next book is available, you can sign up for my new release e-mail list via my website —www.dianafraser.com.

Happy reading!

Diana

PERFECT

BOOK 1 OF ITALIAN ROMANCE—
ALESSANDRO AND EMILY

Falling for the perfectly handsome Alessandro Cavour, Count di
Montecorvio Rovella, is the last thing archaeologist Emily Carlyle
needs as she recovers from the physical and emotional scars

inflicted by an ex-boyfriend. But she can't avoid him when she finds out he owns the estate where she's discovered an ancient Roman site.

Restoring one particular mosaic on the site has become an obsession with Emily – one which Alessandro can't understand. He has no interest in digging up the past because, despite appearances, he bears his own scars. Consumed by guilt over the death of his wife and son, commitment-shy Alessandro lives only for the pleasures of the present. But he hadn't reckoned on falling in love. And love, he discovers, forces difficult choices...

Excerpt

Alessandro pulled back a branch of an overgrown orange tree, its blossom ghostly and its scent overpowering in the twilight.

She turned on the torch and walked past him, her bare arm accidentally touching his.

Her eyes flicked up to his in acknowledgement of the mutual charge that had been ignited before she quickly turned away. He followed her down the tunnel-like path, tamped down by the team of archaeologists, but surrounded by the overgrown trees and undergrowth of centuries of neglect.

She stopped abruptly at the edge of the clearing and he looked around with interest. He remembered it as a child. Despite the overgrown vegetation he'd managed to make a tunnel through to a small part of the ruin. Not that he had been interested in ancient ruins, only in getting out of trouble, of hiding where no-one could find him.

"You know much about all this?"

Her voice was hushed, intimate, in the secluded setting. They were in an enclosed area, surrounded by overgrown shrubbery, and beyond, the dark hills encircled them in absolute secrecy. The tone of her voice seemed to vibrate directly to him across the paved surfaces of the Roman remains, sending a flicker of sensation across his skin.

What was it about this woman that touched him so? She was no seductress. With her large old-fashioned glasses covering her face, her hair drawn back severely, and her boyish shirt, shorts and sandals, she would have been invisible among the crowds of tourists who flocked to Pompeii. He watched her turn in the direction of the mosaic. The strong line of her determined chin, a challenge; the full lips that lay lightly parted, an invitation. She turned, obviously wondering why he did not reply. He cleared his throat and stepped over to her.

"No. It was just a place where one could hide from trouble. The cold marble under your body on a hot day, the trees overhead: a good hiding place. I don't even think my grandparents were aware of it."

She shone the torch on to a small part of the unfinished mosaic depicting a goddess clothed in flowers and gold.

"This is where the lady of the house would have slept. Each of the rooms has a different character. This is the real find. The Aphrodite Mosaic." She approached it and touched it with her fingertips, trailing them over the lumpy surface like a lover. "Isn't it wonderful? They've used all kinds of tesserae to get the subtle colors and shades. It's so delicate, so—."

"Incomplete."

She pursed her lips. "But it won't be. It might have been forgotten about in your parents' and grandparents' time but thanks to your nineteenth-century ancestors we've discovered very fine, detailed drawings that show exactly how it should look. Otherwise, I couldn't do the work. I'm finding whole sections that simply need to be carefully replaced. There are only small parts that need to be filled up from the tiny pieces scattered around here." She stopped suddenly as if conscious that her passion for her work was making her talk too much. "It will be beautiful," she added softly.

Buy Now!

J Laepi — WAXD4K Booking Ref.

MC — WB064G

Rosey — X3157

① Notradame
② Eiffel Tower
③ Louvre
④ Versille
⑤ Lunch Cruise on the Sien river

Buy a 5 day train pass.